Edward S. Ellis

The Young Ranchers

Edward S. Ellis

The Young Ranchers

1st Edition | ISBN: 978-3-73406-227-8

Place of Publication: Frankfurt am Main, Germany

Year of Publication: 2019

Outlook Verlag GmbH, Germany.

THE YOUNG RANCHERS

OR *FIGHTING THE SIOUX*

"FOREST AND PRAIRIE SERIES," No. 3.

BY EDWARD S. ELLIS

AUTHOR OF "BOY PIONEER SERIES," "DEERFOOT SERIES," "WILDWOOD SERIES," ETC.

PHILADELPHIA
HENRY T. COATES & CO.

THE DEATH OF THE FAITHFUL MESSENGER.

CONTENTS.

LIST OF ILLUSTRATIONS

THE YOUNG RANCHERS;

OR,

FIGHTING THE SIOUX.

CHAPTER I.

DANGER AHEAD.

There was snow in the air. Warren Starr had felt it ever since meridian, though not a flake had fallen, and the storm might be delayed for hours yet to come. There was no mistaking the dull leaden sky, the chill in the atmosphere, and that dark, increasing gloom which overspreads the heavens at such times.

Young Warren was a fine specimen of the young hunter, though he had not yet passed his nineteenth year. His home was in South Dakota, and he was now on his return from Fort Meade, at the eastern foot of the Black Hills, and had fully twenty miles to travel, though the sun was low in the horizon, as he well knew, even if it was veiled by the snow vapor.

His father's ranch lay to the north of the Big Cheyenne, and the son was familiar with every foot of the ground, having traversed it many a time, not only on his visits to the fort, but in the numerous hunting excursions of which he was so fond. He could have made the journey by night, when no moon was in the sky, had there been need of doing so, but he decided that it was better to give his pony the rest he required, and to push on at an early hour the next morning. He had eaten nothing since the noon halt, and his youth and vigor gave him a powerful appetite, but he had learned long before that one of the first requisites of the hunter is to learn to endure cold, heat, hunger, and hardship unmurmuringly.

But the youth was in so uneasy a mental state that he rode slowly for nearly an hour, debating with himself whether to draw rein or push on. The rumors of trouble among the Sioux were confirmed by his visit to Fort Meade. A spirit of unrest had prevailed for a long time, caused by the machinations of that marplot, Sitting Bull, the harangues of medicine men who proclaimed the coming Messiah, the ghost dances, the eagerness of the young bucks to take the warpath, and the universal belief that the last opportunity for the red men to turn back the advance of the Caucasian race was to be made soon or never.

The fact that our Government had its military posts scattered through the disaffected country, that the Indian reservations were comparatively well governed, that the officers were men whose valor and skill had been proven times without number, and that these authorities were keeping close watch on the growing disaffection produced a quieting effect in many quarters, though the best informed men foresaw the impending storm. That which troubled Warren Starr on his lonely ride northward was the fact that on that ranch, twenty miles away, dwelt his father, mother, and little sister, known by the pet name of Dot. His father had two assistants in the care of the ranch, Jared Plummer, a man in middle life, and Tim Brophy, a lusty young Irishman, about the same age as Warren. But the ranch was not fitted to withstand an attack from any of the bands through the country. Those turbulent bucks were the very ones to assail his home with the fury of a cyclone, and if they did, Heaven help the loved ones there, even though the three men were well provided with arms and ammunition.

The commandant of Fort Meade suggested to Warren that he urge his people to come into the fort without delay. Such a suggestion, coming from the officer, meant a good deal.

That which caused the youth to decide to wait until morning was the fatigue of his animal, and the more important fact that it was best not only to arrive at the ranch in the daytime, but to ride through several miles of the surrounding country when the chance to use his eyes was at the best. If hostiles were in the section, he might pass within a hundred yards of them in the darkness without discovering it, but it was impossible to do so when the sun was in the sky.

He was now riding across an open plain directly toward a small branch of the Big Cheyenne, beyond which lay his home. He could already detect the fringe of timber that lined both sides of the winding stream, while to the right rose a rocky ridge several hundred feet in height, and a mile or two distant appeared a similar range on the left.

The well-marked trail which the lad was following passed between these elevations; that on the right first presenting itself and diverging so far to the east, just before the other ridge was reached, that it may be said it disappeared, leaving the other to succeed it.

Despite the long ride and the fatigue of himself as well as his animal, young Starr was on the alert. He was in a dangerous country, and a little negligence on his part was liable to prove fatal.

"If there is a lot of Sioux watching this trail for parties going either way, this is the spot," he reflected, grasping his Winchester, lying across his saddle, a little more firmly. "I have met them here more than once, and, though they claimed to be friendly, I was always uneasy, for it is hard for an Indian to resist the temptation to hurt a white man when it looks safe to do so."

Nothing could have exceeded the caution of the youth. The trail showed so plainly that his pony kept to it without any guidance on his part, and the reins lay loose on his neck. Every minute or two the rider glanced furtively behind him to make sure no treacherous enemy was stealing upon him unawares; and then, after a hasty look to the right and left, he scanned the rocky ridge on his right, peering forward the next moment at the one farther off on his left.

He was searching for that which he did not want to find—signs of red men. He knew a good deal of their system of telegraphy, and half suspected that some keen-eyed Sioux was crouching behind the rocks of the ridge, awaiting the moment to signal his approach to his confederate farther away.

It might have seemed possible to some to flank the danger by turning far to the right or left, but that would have involved a long detour and delay in arriving home. At the same time, if any warriors were on the watch, they could easily checkmate him by accommodating their movements to his, and continually heading him off, whichever direction he took. He had considered all these contingencies, and felt no hesitation in pressing straight forward, despite the apparent peril involved in doing so.

Suddenly Jack pricked his ears and raised his head, emitting at the same time a slight whiff through his nostrils.

No words could have said more plainly: "Beware, master! I have discovered something."

The rider's natural supposition was that the danger, whatever it might be, was on the crest of the ridge he was approaching; but, when he shaded his eyes and peered forward, he was unable to detect anything at all. Enough light remained in the sky for him to use his excellent eyes to the best advantage, but nothing rewarded the scrutiny.

Jack continued advancing, though his gait was now a slow walk, as if he expected his master to halt altogether; but the latter acted like the skilful railway engineer, who, seeing the danger signal ahead, continues creeping slowly toward it, ready to check his train on the instant it becomes necessary to do so. He allowed the pony to step tardily forward, while he strove to locate the point whence peril threatened.

"What the mischief do you see, Jack?" he asked, in a half-impatient tone; "if I didn't know you never joked, I would believe you were trying some trick on me to get me to camp for the night."

Once the horseman fancied he caught the faint outlines of a thin column of smoke climbing into the sky from the crest of the ridge, but closer study convinced him that he was wrong. If such a signal were kindled, it must be clear enough to be recognized from the farther elevation, which was more distant than the horseman.

"I shall observe the vapor as soon as they," he thought, "for my eyes are as sharp—helloa! that beats the mischief!"

At last Warren Starr learned what it was that had alarmed his pony.

CHAPTER II.

THE VOICELESS FRIEND.

The keen eyes, instead of looking at the crest of the rocky ridge on his right, were now centred on the ground, where they detected a small dark speck swiftly approaching the horseman. At the first glance, the object suggested a cannon-ball rolling with great speed toward the pony, that was now standing still, with head erect, ears thrown forward, and the appearance of perplexed interest in the thing, whatever it might be.

For a minute Warren Starr was unable to guess the meaning of the singular sight. Whatever its nature, it was evident that it was aiming to reach the rider with the least possible delay. The latter drew his Winchester around in front, so as to be ready to receive it, his first thought being that it was some Sioux stratagem designed to do him ill.

But while he gazed, he discovered its identity; it was a dog, running as if its very life were at stake. The next instant young Starr perceived something protruding from the front part of its body, resembling the ornamental feather in an Indian's head-dress.

"It is an arrow!" he exclaimed. "The poor creature is badly wounded, and is striving to reach me before he dies. By gracious, it's Bruno!" he added, as a closer approach enabled him to identify the creature. "He brings me some message."

Bruno was his favorite hound, that had accompanied him on many a hunting excursion, and whom he loved scarcely less than Jack, his pony.

It was indeed a race with death on the part of the faithful animal. While yet a number of rods distant, he staggered, faltered, then gathering his energies pressed on with the last strength he could summon, and with a low moan rolled languidly on his side, and looking upward with a human expression to his young master, said by his action: "I have done the best I could for you, and I am content."

Young Starr was out of the saddle like a flash, and ran forward to him. Stooping down, he placed one arm under the head of the noble dog, and, leaning over, touched his lips to the velvety forehead.

"My poor Bruno, they have killed you!" he murmured, with tears in his eyes. "I would give an arm to save you, but it is too late."

He saw that the head of the arrow was sunken deep into the neck, and the dark coat was splashed with crimson. To attempt to withdraw the missile was useless. It could only deepen the agony of the animal without relieving him in the least. He was doomed and dying before he sank to the ground.

Bruno turned his beautiful eyes upward to his master, emitted a low moan, gave a slight quiver and gasp, and was dead. No martyr ever did his duty more heroically.

For a few moments Warren Starr yielded to his grief. He remained with the exquisitely formed head resting on his arm, while the tears fell from his eyes on the form that could never respond again to his caresses. Then he gently withdrew his arm and suffered the head to rest on the ground.

"Your last act was for those you love," he murmured; "you gave your life for us, and no man could do more. No one shall take from me the faith that we shall be happy together beyond the grave. Good-by, my true and faithful friend."

Young Starr was too experienced a scout, despite his youth, to forget in his grief the full significance of the sad incident. The hound had travelled the long distance from the ranch to this point for the purpose of bringing him a message. He had been discovered while on the road, and fired upon by the Indians, who were so near that they used bows and arrows to prevent the young master taking the alarm. Many missiles were doubtless sent after the animal, and one was fated to bring him down, though not until he had accomplished his errand.

Warren knew where to look for the message. He unstrapped the collar, with its silver plate—which he would have done under any circumstance to keep as a remembrance of his voiceless friend—and there, carefully folded and secure under the band, was a piece of paper, containing considerable writing in lead-pencil:

DEAR WARREN:

Don't come to the ranch. It is sure death to undertake it. A party of twenty and more bucks are near us. They have killed or stampeded our cattle, and will attack us this evening if we remain, which we shall not do. Tim discovered them this afternoon, and learned enough to make sure of their intention. We shall mount our horses and start for Fort Meade. We dare not use the regular trail, along which I suppose you are making your way, but must be guided by circumstances. I think we shall move to the westward, taking the most direct route to the post, but are likely to be forced into a long detour, which renders it impossible for me to give you any direction by which we can meet each other.

I know that your impulse will be to try to join us before we reach the fort, but it is my earnest wish that you shall not attempt it. Turn about at once, while you have time, and retrace your steps. If a day or two shall pass without our coming in, perhaps it may be well to ask the colonel to send out a squad of cavalry to help us, for it is idle to fancy we are not in great peril. It is my prayer that Bruno shall intercept you in time to prevent any mishap. I have instructed him precisely what he is expected to do, and he not only fully understands, but, as you well know, will do it if it be possible.

YOUR FATHER.

"You were right," said the youth gently, looking down once more on the inanimate form. "Bruno did his duty, and he deserves a monument for having done it so well."

All this time the pony stood some feet away, motionless, and apparently a deeply interested witness of the singular scene.

He was too well trained to leave his master, who never resorted to the precaution of securing him by his halter.

Meanwhile night was closing in. The gloom was overspreading the prairie so that the ridge, which had been such a cause for solicitude to the youth, was now dimly discernible. In a few minutes it would be swallowed up in the coming darkness.

Resolutely forcing his sadness aside, Warren knelt down and pressed his ear to the ground. If horsemen were approaching he could detect it through the sense of hearing.

Then he climbed once more into the saddle and faced the ridge, debating with himself what was the right course to pursue. His father had said in unmistakable language that he wished him to return to Fort Meade. Warren was a dutiful son, but he could not persuade himself that that was the best thing to do. To follow his parent's wishes would require him to look after his own safety, and to forget those whose lives were dearer to him than his own. To return to the fort, and secure the aid that he knew would be cheerfully given, would take a day or two, during which the crisis must come and pass with his people. Two days at the most would settle the question whether they were to escape or fall victims to the ferocity of the Sioux.

"I can't do it," he said, compressing his lips and shaking his head. "I have never played the coward, and I'm not going to begin when my folks are concerned. My first duty is to find out where father, mother, and Dot are, and then do all I can for their safety."

It was not difficult to reach this conclusion, for which no one will deny him credit; but it was altogether a difficult and formidable task for him to decide what next to do.

Had his friends been following the regular trail to the fort his course would have been simple, since he had only to continue on until he met them; but his father had notified him that not only would he not take that route, but he could not say which one he would adopt. He inclined to think he would turn to the westward, leaving the path on his left, but the question, as he said, must be settled by circumstances.

Something cold touched his hand. It was a snowflake, and he knew that in a short time the ground would be wrapped in a mantle of white. Once more he glanced in the direction of the elevation, now invisible in the gathering darkness. On the utmost height a point of light appeared, shining for a moment with the steady radiance of a fixed star.

"The bucks are there," concluded Warren; "they saw me from a long way, and must wonder why I am delayed—ah, sure enough!"

All at once the gleaming light began circling about, faster and faster, until it looked like a wheel of fire. Then it reversed, whirling as swiftly in the opposite direction, then up and down, then from side to side, and finally, whiff! it vanished.

A grim smile lit the face of the youth, who turned his gaze toward the more distant ridge on his left for the answer, but if it was made, the state of the atmosphere prevented his seeing it. Once he fancied he caught the glimpse of something resembling a fire-fly, but it was only for an instant, and was not observed again.

It was easy to read the meaning of that which first showed itself. A party of Indians that had evidently been watching his coming, while yet a long way off, now telegraphed his arrival to their confederates on the more distant elevation, together with the fact that the white man had ceased his approach and might not come any nearer.

It was reasonable to believe that these same red men would not remain idle while the object of their wrath turned quietly about and retraced his steps.

Only a few minutes were used in considering the question, but the time had not yet expired, when, to Warren's astonishment, he heard the sound of firing ahead. Probably eight or ten shots were discharged at quick but irregular intervals, and then all once more became still.

A pang of apprehension passed through him at the fear that his friends, after all, might have attempted to reach the fort by the trail, and had become involved in a fight with the Sioux. Be that as it may, the fact was impressed on him that he was doing an imprudent thing by remaining in the path along which the warriors were liable to burst at any moment. He turned Jack to the left and rode fully a hundred yards before again drawing rein. It was not necessary to go this far to place himself beyond sight of the path, but he wished to take no unnecessary chances.

By this time the snowflakes were falling fast, and it was impossible to see objects more than twenty feet distant. Warren checked his pony, holding him with his nose toward the trail, and listened.

Again the intelligent animal elevated his head, pricked his ears, and emitted an almost noiseless neigh, as was his habit when he discovered the approach of strangers. His rider could discern nothing through the gloom, and resorted to the resource tried before, which is a common one among hunters and warriors. Descending from the saddle, he brushed aside the snow from a small spot on the ground and pressed his ear against the earth.

This time he *did* hear something. A horse was approaching over the trail on a swift gallop, and it took but a brief while for the youth to learn that he was coming from the direction of the ridge. Furthermore, there was but the single horseman; or, if there were others, they were so far off that no thought need be given to them.

Remounting his pony, Warren held him facing the path, and prepared for any emergency likely to arise. He was well aware that if the stranger kept to the trail he would be invisible in the gloom, but he was now so near that from his seat young Starr plainly caught the sound of his horse's hoofs, growing more distinct every moment.

Whoever it was that was advancing, it was evident he was doing so at what might be called a leisurely pace, though it was quite rapid. The horse was on an easy canter, such as his species can maintain for hours without fatigue.

The youth was sitting in this posture, with never a thought of what was coming, when to his amazement he caught the outlines of the man and his steed passing at right angles to the course he had been following himself.

"He is off the trail!" was the alarming fact which caused Warren to make ready to fire, for the truth was apparent that if he saw the stranger, the latter had the same opportunity of seeing him.

To his surprise Jack uttered a neigh at the critical moment when the other was directly opposite. A collision now seemed certain, but the other kept straight on, and quickly passed from sight.

Not until he had been several minutes beyond hearing did the startling thought come to Warren Starr:

"That was a white man, and not an Indian."

CHAPTER III.

COMPANIONS IN PERIL.

Warren Starr was impatient with himself that he had not thought of the stranger being a white man until it was too late to make use of the important fact. The sounds of firing ahead ought to have raised the suspicion in his mind, and the act of his pony should have confirmed it, for he never would have betrayed himself to one of his own species had he not known that he belonged to a friend.

But it was a waste of time to bewail what could not be helped, and nothing was to be gained by staying where he was. There was no longer any call to push onward toward the ranch, for that was not his destination. He was seeking his folks.

Once more the nose of Jack was turned about, and this time he was headed toward the northwest, his course being such that it would take him considerably to the west of the second rocky ridge to which allusion has been made. In short, Warren had now set out to do that which he would not have attempted but for the receipt of the message from his father. He was about to flank both elevations by swerving far from the direct course to his home.

The small tributary of the Big Cheyenne, which it was necessary to ford in order to reach the ranch, made a sweeping curve southward, so that the marked change in the course he was following would take him to it, though at a point far removed from the regular ford.

The youth was not riding blindly forward. It has been stated that he was familiar with the country for many miles around his home, and he was making for a definite point. It was on the bank of the small stream, and was not only deeply wooded, but abounded with rocks, bowlders, depressions, ravines, and wild, dangerous places, where it was certain death for a person to try to make his way in the darkness, unless he knew every foot of the locality.

This was the locality for which young Starr was aiming. Here he was confident of finding security against the Sioux, though they might be near at hand. He knew just where to go, for he had hunted through it many times with his friend Tim Brophy, for whose company he longed more than ever before.

Jack wanted food, but it could not be had. He did not need it, however, to the extent of suffering. At the noon halt, when his master sat on the ground by a spring of cold water to eat his lunch, the pony had cropped the succulent grass that grew around, and he could stand it quite well until the morrow. The animal needed rest and shelter more than anything else, and it was that which his young master meant he should have.

As if he understood it all, the horse of his own accord struck into a brisk gallop, which rendered unnecessary any other protection from the cold. The snow was still falling, but the temperature was not low, and there was not enough on the ground to interfere with the travelling of the animal, who maintained his pace until the abrupt appearance of the rocky section, with its trees and bowlders, compelled him to drop to a slow walk, with his nose thrust forward, as if to scent every step of the way, like an elephant crossing a doubtful bridge.

"Here we are, my boy!" called out Warren, "and you couldn't have come more truly if the sun had been shining."

It certainly was a marvellous piece of woodcraft, if such it may be called, on the part of the pony, that he should have struck the spot so accurately, and yet it is scarcely less marvellous that, had he needed direction, his master was competent to give it, despite the darkness and the snow.

Warren left the saddle for the last time. With no stars or moon in the sky, and with the snow falling faster than ever, it would seem that one's eyes were of little use, but they served their purpose well in the present instance. Paying no heed to the animal, he bent over, groping his way among the rocks, which began abruptly on the edge of the prairie, and had not spent five minutes thus when he came upon that for which he was looking—an opening between a mass of bowlders, along which a person or animal could make his way with little difficulty.

"Here we are, Jack, my boy! Come on; we'll soon reach our house."

With more thrusting forward of the head, and sniffing of the air, the pony obeyed, though it is hardly to be supposed that he understood all that was said to him.

On the previous winter, when Warren Starr and Tim Brophy were hunting in this section, they found game so abundant that they decided to spend two or three days in the neighborhood. Accordingly they put up a shelter which afforded good protection at night, and would do the same against any storm not too violent. A rock a dozen feet in length formed a half-circle, the upper edge projecting over to the extent of a yard or more. All that was required was to lean a number of branches against this, the upper parts supported by the ledge, while the lower rested on the ground, some eight or ten feet away from the base.

These branches being numerous and thickly placed, constituted what might be considered a tepee, with only the broad opening in front.

It was in this rude shelter that Warren Starr and Tim Brophy had spent a couple of nights in comparative comfort. The second one was bitterly cold, and they kindled a fire near the entrance. The smoke caused some trouble, but wrapped in their thick blankets, and stretched out back to back, they slept as soundly as if in their beds at home.

This was the structure which the youth had in mind when he turned his back on the regular trail and made for the wild solitude through which he now began threading his way, and it was a striking tribute to his woodcraft and knowledge that within fifteen minutes he reached the very spot, with his pony at his heels.

"This is the place," he remarked to his animal, "but there don't seem to be any lamps lighted, and it's best to look around a little before retiring for the night."

Drawing a rubber match-safe from his pocket, he ignited one of the tiny bits of wood, shading the twist of flame from the snowflakes, though there was no wind stirring.

It was months since he had visited the place, and the elements were likely to have played havoc with the structure during that period, for in that part of our Union the blizzard and tempest raise the mischief at certain seasons.

He was gratified, however, to note the slight change effected. One or two of the long branches had fallen to the ground and several others were askew. He was obliged to fling aside the match while he devoted some minutes to straightening them. This was effected so well that when he stepped inside and struck another match he saw not a flake of snow filtering through the crevices, though there was likely to be considerable before morning.

"Come in!" was the astonishing command the youth gave to his pony, who stood looking at him, as if wondering what the next move was to be. The situation was amusing, and not without its ludicrous side, with Warren holding a match in one hand, his rifle in the other, and his heavy blanket wrapped about his shoulders, beckoning and addressing the pony, which hesitated for a minute at this unexpected invitation to share the couch of his master.

But he was an obedient animal, and with some more sniffing and poking forward of his nose, he stepped slowly forward until he was entirely within the rude structure.

"Now lie down," added Warren, lighting another match, and Jack obeyed with more promptness than before. Then the youth flung the broad, heavy blanket over the pony so as to envelop as much of him as possible, lay down close to the front of his body, adjusting the hoofs as best he could, drew the rest of the covering over himself, and was excusable for chuckling:

"Now, Jack, old fellow, what's to prevent us from sleeping as snug as a bug in a rug! Hey, my boy?"

Everything promised well, but before either could fall asleep, they were startled beyond measure by hearing someone moving outside. Whispering to the horse to keep still, Warren slipped out from under the blanket and moved softly to the opening, revolver in hand. As he did so, he ran squarely against another person who was in the act of entering the place of shelter.

CHAPTER IV.

TIM BROPHY'S DISCOVERY.

The letter which was delivered to Warren Starr by his mortally wounded hound not only gave that young man definite news of the alarming events in the neighborhood of his home, but has conveyed to the reader the cause of the abrupt change in his plans and of the stirring incidents which led to the hasty flight of the Starr family from their ranch on the north of the Big Cheyenne River.

As stated in the note, it was Tim Brophy, the young Irishman, who made the discovery in time to prevent the family being overwhelmed and massacred. While Jared Plummer, the lank New Englander, rode to the westward to look after some strays, Tim galloped north to attend to the main herd, which was supposed to be cropping the abundant grass in the neighborhood of several small streams and tributaries of the main river.

Tim had been in the employ of Mr. Starr for three years, and had spent most of his life in the West, so that he had fully learned the lesson which such an experience should teach everyone. He knew of the impending trouble among the Indian tribes, and was always on the alert. It was not long, therefore, before he came upon signs which told him something was amiss.

In the corner of a natural clearing, near one of the small streams, he discovered a dozen of the cattle lying dead. It was not necessary for him to dismount and examine the ground to learn the cause of such slaughter. The footprints of ponies near by, the bullet wounds, and other indications answered the question that came to his lips at the first glimpse of the cruel butchery.

"The spalpeens!" he exclaimed wrath-fully. "They niver had a better friend than Mr. Starr, and that's the shtyle in which they pays him for the same. Worrah, worrah, but it's too bad!"

Riding cautiously to the top of the next elevation, the young rancher saw other sights which filled him with greater indignation and resentment. A half mile to the northward the entire herd of cattle, numbering several hundreds, were scurrying over the plain in a wild panic. The figures of several Sioux bucks galloping at their heels, swinging their arms and shouting, so as to keep up and add to the affright, left no doubt that Mr. Starr's fine drove of cattle was gone beyond recovery. The result of months of toil, expense, and trouble were vanishing as they sometimes do before the resistless sweep of the cyclone.

The blue eyes of the Celt flashed, as he sat in the saddle and contemplated the exasperating raid. Nothing would have pleased him better than to dash with several companions after the marauders and force them to a reckoning for the outrage. But eager as he was for such an affray, he was too wise to try it alone. There were five or six of the horsemen, and he was no match for them.

Besides this, a more alarming discovery broke upon him within a minute after observing the stampede. From the clump of wood on his right, along the edge of the stream, only a few hundred yards away, he detected the faint smoke of a camp-fire. The Sioux were there.

The sight so startled Tim that he wheeled his pony short around and withdrew behind the elevation he had just ascended, fearing he had already been observed by the red men.

Such undoubtedly would have been the fact had any of the turbulent Sioux been on guard, but the occasion was one of those rare ones in which the warriors acted upon the theory that no such precaution was needed, since no possible danger could threaten them.

Suspecting the truth, Tim dropped hastily from his pony and stole along the edge of the stream, until he reached a point which gave him a sight of the miscreants, and at the same time afforded him tolerably fair protection.

The scene was calculated to inspire anything but pleasant feelings in a spectator. Fully a score of young warriors were squatted in a circle, listening to the harangue of one of their number, who had wrought himself into a furious passion. He was swinging his arms, shouting and leaping about like a lunatic, and rising to a pitch which not only threatened to throw him into a paroxysm, but was imparting itself to his listeners. Some of them were smoking, but showing at the same time an excitement which is generally believed to be foreign to the American race. They were all bucks, and eager to be led upon the warpath. There was not an old or middle-aged man among them.

The eavesdropper was not able to understand their words, but the gestures left no doubt of their fearful meaning. The speaker pointed in the direction of the home of the Starrs so often, and indulged in so much action to which the others signified full assent, that it was beyond dispute that they meant to attack the house and slay the inmates. Knowing all about these, and the resistance they were likely to meet, they would wait until night before bursting upon them.

Tim Brophy was sagacious enough to grasp almost on the instant the full nature of the awful peril. He saw that accident, or rather Providence, had given to him the secret which revealed that only by prompt action could the lives of his friends be saved. There was no saying how long the council, if such it may be called, would last, and he did not care to know.

Nothing could show the intense absorption of the fierce Sioux in the outrage they had determined to commit more than the fact that a white man rose up in full view only a few hundred yards away, without his presence being detected. Such being the case, it was easy for Tim to withdraw from the immediate vicinity of the gathering, steal round to where his pony was cropping the grass, and mount again.

He rode carefully forward, keeping the elevation between him and the camp of the hostiles, until convinced it was safe, when he struck his horse into a run and sped away as if for life.

A few minutes sufficed to take him to the house, where the unsuspicious folk looked up in wonder at his haste and agitation. Mr. Starr was sitting near the window reading a newspaper, his little girl Dot was playing with her doll on the floor, and the wife was busy with her household duties.

It took but a few minutes for Tim to tell the news. Jared Plummer had not yet come in, and there could be no guessing as to what additional facts he would give them.

Like his employé, the rancher was quick to grasp the situation. The only possible safety was in flight, and no time was to be lost.

The building, with its broad, flat roof, its many windows and insecure portions, was in no condition for successful defence, where the small garrison could not guard one-half the weak points. The assailants could readily fire it, and it would burn like so much touchwood. Flight, therefore, was the one and only thing to be thought of.

It was yet comparatively early in the afternoon, and those on the ranch had noted the signs of the approaching snowstorm. The husband directed his wife to make her preparations few and simple, and to waste no time. It was idle to bewail the necessity which compelled them to leave so many precious articles behind. Life was dearer than all, and the courageous helpmate proved herself equal to the occasion. She gathered the articles of clothing they were likely to need, filled several bags with the provisions in the house, and announced that she was ready.

There was a horse each for the father, mother, and Tim Brophy, while a fourth, a small, tough pony, was laden with the bag of provisions, extra clothing, and a few articles deemed indispensable. These were brought round to the front, and in much less time than would be supposed the little cavalcade was ready to move.

Despite the belief of Brophy that no attack would be made until after darkness had closed,—a belief shared by Mr. Starr,—the rancher was fearful that his home would be placed under surveillance while daylight lasted, and that the intended flight would be discovered before it began. In such an event, the family could only fight it out to the desperate end, and that they would do so admits of no doubt.

CHAPTER V.

LEAVING THE RANCH.

Now that everything was ready, Mr. Starr felt anxious about the absent Jared Plummer. He ought to have learned of the danger before this, and should have been almost, if not quite, as prompt as Tim Brophy in hastening to the house. His continued absence gave ground for fear that harm had befallen him, but his friends were powerless to give him help.

"It won't do to wait," remarked the rancher gravely, "and he will be as able to do without as with us."

"Why not lave a missage for him?" asked Tim.

"The idea is a good one," replied Mr. Starr, who, sitting down, hurriedly penned the following upon a slip of paper, and pinned it on the front door of the dwelling, where it was sure to catch the eye of the absent one in the event of his return:

To Jared Plummer:

The presence of the Sioux, and the certainty that they will attack the ranch before long, leave no choice for us but to flee at once. I have waited as long as I dare. We shall take a south-west course and will aim to reach Fort Meade. Follow as soon as you can, and we will look out for each other; but give your thoughts and energies to taking care of yourself. More than likely we shall not see each other until we meet at the post, if it be God's will that we shall safely arrive there.

George Starr.

Little Dot watched her father with great interest while he was fastening this piece of paper to the door of their home.

"What's that for, papa?" she asked.

"It is something for Mr. Plummer to read when he comes back."

"Don't you want anyone else to read it?"

"Of course not," replied the parent with a smile, lovingly patting the chubby cheek.

"But if the bad Indians you and mamma have been talking about come here, they will read it too."

The father started. He had not thought of that. The next moment, however, he laughed.

"The Indians don't know how to read writing or print, so it won't do them any good."

"But Starcus can read as well as anybody."

"He has been to school and learned, and then he is a good Indian, too, and I wouldn't care if he did read it."

"But maybe he will become bad like the other Indians," persisted the child.

The husband looked significantly at his wife, who was also watching his actions and listening to the conversation. She replied with a motion of the head, which said there might be something in the words of the little one.

Starcus was a young Indian that had been attending the Carlisle school for a couple of years, and had acquired a fair English education, being able to read, write, and talk intelligently. He had called at the house several times, and interested the family by his pleasing ways and kind words.

He remarked on his last visit, some weeks before, that he was likely to remain some time with his people, and possibly would not return again to the East. Many things were more unlikely than that he would be carried away by the craze that was affecting his tribe, and become one of the most ferocious foes of the Caucasian race.

"Tim," said Mr. Starr, turning to the Irishman, "did you notice whether he was among the group you saw?"

"I didn't observe him, but they were fixed out in war-paint and toggery so that I wouldn't have knowed the gintleman onless I was inthrodooced to the same. Thin, too, he might have been one of the spalpeens who were stampeding the cattle."

"Well, there's no use in thinking of that; we must take the chances; the Sioux will find out what course we follow without asking anyone to translate this message for them."

Mrs. Starr caught the arm of her husband, and as he turned he noticed that her face was pale with emotion.

"What is it, wife?" he asked in alarm.

"Warren," she replied in a whisper.

"What about him?"

"This is the day he said he would leave the fort for home; he must be on the way now; unless he is warned he will ride to his death without suspecting it."

The father forgot their own danger for the moment in his alarm for his son. It took but a few minutes to act upon the plan of which the reader has learned long since. Another letter was pencilled and secured to the collar of Bruno, whose instructions were so minute that they would have been ludicrous, but for their warrant in the wonderful intelligence of the animal. The hound sped away like an arrow from the bow, and the faithfulness with which he did his work need not be retold.

There was no call for further delay. Mr. Starr mounted his fine animal, armed with Winchester and revolver, after he had assisted his wife upon another horse and placed Dot in front of her. The mother was a superior horsewoman, and this arrangement was intended to leave the husband free to act without hinderance, in the event of an emergency. Tim Brophy was equally at liberty, and with the pack animal well laden the party left the home, each oppressed by a great fear that they would not only never look upon it again, but would probably be struck down before reaching the nearest point of safety, many miles away, at the base of the Black Hills.

More than one eye anxiously turned toward the elevation, beyond which Tim Brophy had seen the bucks listening to the impassioned harangue of their leader, and the relief was not great when they rode over another swell in the plain, which shut them out from the sight of any of the serpent-eyed Sioux concealed there; for there could be no certainty that the fugitives had not been observed by them. It was not the custom of their people to attack openly; more likely they would set some ambush into which the whites might ride with no thought of danger.

But in one sense the Rubicon was crossed. They had turned their backs on the ranch, and it was to be dismissed from their thoughts until they should reach some place of safety.

There was little said by any member of the party, for the occasion was not one to induce conversation. Even little Dot was oppressed by the general gloom, and nestled close to her mother, whose arm lovingly encircled and held her close to her breast, which would gladly receive any blow intended for that precious one.

Tim Brophy remained a brief distance at the rear, with the pack animal, on the alert for the first sign of danger, while Mr. Starr gave his attention to the front, selecting the course, and doing all in his power to avoid leading his companions into danger.

When, however, a half mile had been passed, during which several ridges were crossed, a feeling of hope arose that after all they might elude their vengeful enemies. With the coming of night, it would be impossible for the Sioux to trail them. They must wait until the following morning, and before that time the fugitives ought to be so near Fort Meade that the pursuit would be in vain.

It was a striking proof of parental affection that now, when the cloud was partly lifted from the father and mother, their anxiety should be transferred to the absent son on his way to join them. He was in the minds of both, and despite his exceptional skill in woodcraft, the conviction grew upon the parents that he was in greater peril than they. Finally, the mother uttered the thoughts in her mind.

"I agree with you, Molly," the husband replied. "Bruno will do his best, but I believe the chances are a hundred to one that he will fail, and Warren will ride straight to his death."

"Can't we do something, George?"

The husband turned his head, and beckoned to his employé to ride up between them.

"Tim, you know the regular trail to the fort as well as the way to your own bedroom. I want you to set out to meet Warren, and prevent his running into the hands of the Sioux."

"Whin would ye like me to start?"

"Now."

"I'm riddy and waiting to ride to me death for the boy, if nade be."

CHAPTER VI.

"TIMOTHY BROPHY, ESQ., AT YOUR SERVICE."

At first thought, the abrupt departure of Tim Brophy may seem an imprudent thing, since it left only one man to look after the safety of Mrs. Starr and their little one; but it will be remembered that the hope of safety lay not in fighting, but in flight; and the presence or absence of the young Irishman could not affect that one way or the other.

Accordingly, with a pause only long enough to draw a substantial lunch from the provision bag and to bid his friends good-by, Tim wheeled his horse and was off like a shot. He took good care to avoid the neighborhood of the bucks, and soon left the ranch far behind, speeding along the trail over which Warren Starr was at that moment galloping toward him.

The youth drove his task through with all the impetuosity of his nature. He was devotedly attached to the son of his employer, and was ready at any time, as he had always been, to risk his life for him. Believing as he did that he was in more imminent peril than anyone else, he bent every energy toward reaching and turning him aside before it was too late.

In this essay, Tim committed a mistake which Warren Starr narrowly avoided. He acted on the theory that the only real danger was in the immediate neighborhood of the ranch, and that none existed near the ridges between which the trail led. The consequence was that, when he was not dreaming of any such thing, he suddenly became the target for a fusillade from Sioux rifles that were waiting to receive young Starr, and therefore were not fully prepared for him. By desperate work and good fortune he and his pony ran the gauntlet unscathed, and continued their flight southward. The whinny of his friend's pony, he supposed, came from one of the horses of his enemies, and therefore he galloped on without paying any heed to it.

Meanwhile, as will be remembered, young Starr had pushed through the falling snow and gathering darkness until he and his horse reached the primitive shelter among the rocks, bowlders, and trees which he had used when on previous hunting expeditions. After he and Jack had disposed themselves for the night they were disturbed by the approach of someone. Rising to his feet, Warren hurried stealthily to the door, where he ran directly against the intruder, whom he was unable to recognize in the gloom.

"Who are you?" he asked, holding his revolver ready for instant use, but unwilling to fire until sure he was facing an enemy.

"Timothy Brophy, Esq., at your service," replied his friend, identifying the other by his voice.

"Why, Tim, I can't tell you how glad I am to see you," exclaimed the delighted Warren: "I have thought a score of times, when on the way, how pleasant it would be to meet you. What brought you here?"

"My horse, and I presume that yours did the same for yersilf."

"Where is he?"

"Outside, near by, wid the bist shelter I could give him: I didn't saa your own."

"He's inside, sharing my couch with me, or, rather, was doing so when you disturbed us."

Tim broke into laughter.

"That's a good idaa; I niver heerd of anything like it before. Is there room for Billy, too?"

"I'm afraid we would be crowded; but come inside till I strike a match and show you how things are fixed."

The two entered, and Warren ignited another lucifer. Jack was evidently puzzled, raising his head and looking at them in a way which suggested that he would like to come to his feet.

"Lie down, old fellow!" commanded his master; "there's nothing to be disturbed about; you couldn't have better quarters, and you will be wise to stay where you are; you're better off than Billy."

Now that Tim had arrived with his blanket, it was decided that the pony should be left where he was, while the youths lay down on the other covering, which was wrapped about them.

Then they curled up and made themselves as comfortable as on their previous stay in the rude shelter.

Lying thus, they naturally talked over what had taken place since their last meeting. Warren's voice trembled when he told the story of Bruno, who gave his life for him and his friends, and Tim related what had befallen the others during the day.

Young Starr was filled with alarm for his parents and little sister, but Tim was hopeful that everything would come out right, and that, by the time the sun rose, they would be so far advanced on their way to Fort Meade that the danger would be virtually over.

"Ye knows," he continued, "that yer fayther is acquainted wid the way as well as yerself; the horses are frish and strong, and he'll not spare thim; the road, too, is not as long as by the rig'lar route that we've follyed so often."

"That is true, but it must be all of thirty miles, and is really much greater because of the ridges, hills, streams, and difficult places in the path, which will compel many detours."

"And the same will have to be observed by the spalpeens that may be thrying to overtake thim."

"But they understand the business better."

"I'm not so sartin of that," sturdily replied Tim; "yer fayther is no green hand."

"That isn't what I mean; I'm thinking of mother and Dot; he will have to accommodate himself to them, and in case the Indians do come up with them _____"

"Arrah, now, what are ye thinking of?" demanded Tim impatiently; "if ye want to go to specylatin' and 'ifing,' ye may refar to oursilves and say that if the spalpeens come down here wid Sitting Bull laading the same, and they sit fire to this ilegant risidence, what will become of us?"

"That is very well, Tim, and you mean right, but I shall not rest a minute until I know they have reached the fort. It's strange, too, about Plummer."

"It's my opinion," remarked the Irishman, lowering his voice, as though afraid of being overheard, "that he's in throuble."

"Why do you think so?"

"Because he did not show up before we lift; he hadn't any farther to go than mesilf, and it was nearly an hour after I got back before we come away, but there was no sign of him."

"Did you hear no firing?"

"Not that I remember; which reminds me that it was also quaar that the Sioux could have shot down the cattle as they did, so near the house, widout any of us noting the noise of their guns."

"It was singular, but perhaps you were all inside at the time, busy at something. At any rate, instead of our hurrying back to the fort, we will do our best to find father and mother, and stick by them to the end."

"I'm wid ye there," was the hearty response of Tim; "I'd like to give Plummer a helping hand, but see no way to do the same, and it is likely that he can get along better widout us than wid us."

The two talked a long time, for their hearts were full. It was not until midnight that a feeling of drowsiness began creeping over them. Tim's remarks began to grow slower and more disconnected, until finally he failed to answer at all. Finding that he was asleep, Warren composed himself as comfortably as he could, and soon joined him in the land of dreams.

The snow continued sifting softly downward, and rattled against the branches and leaves which composed a portion of their house. The temperature sank as the night progressed, and the situation of the couple, no less than that of their friends, became anything but hopeful.

They were still a long way from the post, where they could feel secure, and the Indians were certain to press them hard. They were so much more numerous than the little band of fugitives that the advantage lay wholly with them.

But the night passed without disturbance. Then the pony and the two youths awoke simultaneously, for they were aroused by one of the most startling causes that can be conceived: It was the screaming whinny of Tim Brophy's horse—a cry rarely heard from the animal, and only when in the very extremity of mortal terror.

CHAPTER VII.

STIRRING TIMES.

Warren Starr and Tim Brophy sprang up at the same instant. The gray light of the early wintry morning was stealing through the rocky solitude, the snow had ceased falling, and the weather was colder than on the preceding evening. The pony also began struggling to his feet, but the youths in their excitement paid no heed to him.

"It's Billy," whispered Tim.

"Yes; let's see what is the matter."

The young Irishman had formed the decision a moment before, for he was as ready to defend his horse as a friend. He bounded out from the rude shelter, with his companion at his heels.

It was but a short distance to the spot where he had left the animal to spend the night. The boys dropped their blankets, but each grasped his Winchester, confident that there was call for its use.

It was on a small natural clearing, where, after grazing a few minutes in the dark, the pony had lain down to sleep, his instinct leading him to select the side of a towering rock, where he was well protected from the falling snow. This bare place was less than a quarter of an acre in extent, and narrowed to what might be called a point, where the horse had found refuge from the storm. Surrounded by bowlders, varying in height from eight or more feet to twice that extent, his only means of entering or leaving was through the opening at the extreme end, which was not less than a rod in width.

The pony had probably risen to his feet with the first coming of daylight, when he was confronted by the most terrifying sight conceivable; a colossal grizzly bear stood in the middle of the "door," calmly surveying him, and evidently of the belief that he had come upon the most palatable kind of breakfast, which was already secured to him beyond possibility of loss.

When it is borne in mind that the pony was caught in a trap as secure as an iron cage, it will be understood why the intelligent animal, in the agony of helplessness, emitted that astounding cry which rang like the wail of doom through the snowy solitude. Thousands of his species live for years and die without giving expression to that horrible outcry, for it requires the agony of fear to call it forth.

The horse has five times the intelligence of the bear, but the latter was not stupid enough to fail to see his advantage, or to allow it to slip from him. The enormous trail which he had made in the snow was noticed by Tim Brophy before seeing the brute, and he identified it at a glance, his only fear being that he might arrive too late to save his pony.

The latter cowered against the rock, his fright so pitiable that, in the stirring moments, both youths were touched with sympathy for him.

"Begorra, but isn't he a bouncer?" whispered Tim, coming to a halt. "I niver looked upon as big a one."

"Has he hurt Billy?" asked Warren, who, as will be remembered, was a few paces behind him while making the brief run.

"He has scared him out of ten years' growth, and it's mesilf that's going to pay the same compliment to the spalpeen."

"Be careful, Tim! You know how hard it is to kill one of those creatures, and when they are roused——"

Further utterance was cut short by the report of Tim's gun. The young Irishman's failing was his impetuosity. When he saw his services needed, he was so eager to give them that he frequently threw caution to the winds, and plunged into the fray like a diver going off the rocks.

Halting less than fifty feet away, he brought his rifle to a level and let fly. It was as impossible for him to miss as it was to inflict a mortal wound, and the ball meant for the skull of the brute found lodgment elsewhere.

The bear appeared to be in the act of rising partly on his haunches, when the report, and probably a sharp twinge in his shoulder, apprised him of what was going on at the rear. The contemplated feast was not to be without its unpleasant interruption.

He uttered a low growl and came straight for the two youths. Their rifles being of the magazine kind, they were prepared to open a bombardment, which they did without delay; but after a number of shots had been fired, and the mountainous animal continued to sweep down upon them, Warren called out:

"Let's run, Tim! we need a cannon to stop him; we must find some place to shelter us."

Not doubting that his comrade would instantly follow, Warren wheeled about and dashed off without paying heed to the direction; he had no time to make any calculations.

Despite the fall of snow, there were only two or three inches on the ground, just enough to interfere with rapid travelling. Young Starr had not taken a dozen steps, when his foot turned on a smooth stone and he pitched headlong, with his gun flying from his grasp. He was not hurt, and he bounded up again as if made of rubber. He supposed the animal, which can lumber along at a speedy gait despite its awkwardness, was on his heels, but the furtive glance over his shoulder showed nothing of him, and the youth plunged forward and caught up his weapon as may be said on the fly.

With its recovery came something like confidence again, and he turned about to learn how Tim Brophy was making out.

It was just like the plucky fellow not to dash after his comrade, but to stand his ground, when the most experienced and the bravest hunter in the world would have lost no time in increasing the distance between him and the brute. The latter had scared Billy half to death, and his master meant to punish him therefor, so he held his ground, and managed to send in another shot while the grizzly was approaching, but which did no more to check his charge than a wad from a pop-gun.

This reckless daring on the part of Tim would have brought disaster, but for an unexpected interference.

Billy, the pony, no sooner saw the terrible brute turn his back upon him and lumber off, than he understood that the way of escape for him had opened. His panic departed like a flash, and he plunged through the opening with a snort of triumph; but his line of flight took him of necessity along that followed by the grizzly himself, who was advancing to the assault of the brave young Irishman.

There may have been a feeling of wrathful resentment thrilling the nerves of the gallant pony, or it is not beyond belief that he understood the danger of his master. Be that as it may, he was no sooner beside the huge brute, who slightly turned his head on hearing the clatter of the hoofs, than he let drive with both hind feet, landing them with such terrific force against the iron ribs of the monster that he fell half upon his side, after being driven several feet beyond the path.

"Good for you!" called the delighted Tim, "let him have another broadside, Billy, and we'll finish him——"

The assault of the pony diverted the attention of the grizzly for a moment from the youth to the assailant. He was thoroughly roused, and made for the horse, who showed more sense than his master by dashing off at full speed. This being beyond the attainment of the bear, it may be said that Billy's escape was absolute.

The sudden check in Tim's words was caused by bruin, who had passed but a few paces beyond the youth, when, seeing how useless it was to pursue the pony, he wheeled and once more charged upon the master.

The moment had arrived for the young rancher to call his legs into service. He was willing to run when the necessity was apparent, and none could excel him as a sprinter—that is, none of his kind.

He assuredly would have been overtaken before he could climb any of the bowlders or rocks, or get out of the path, had not a bullet bored its way directly through the brain of the grizzly, and brought him to earth at the moment when the life of the fugitive hung on a thread.

CHAPTER VIII.

STARCUS.

Warren Starr was terrified for the moment by the peril of his companion. While running toward him he saw the grizzly rise partly on his haunches to seize Tim, who was within his grasp, but at that instant the brute toppled over, and with one or two struggles was dead.

It was an exciting moment, but a singular discovery came to young Starr—the shot that slew the bear was fired neither by himself nor Tim!

Without waiting to investigate, he dashed to where his panting friend was looking down at the fallen monster, as if uncertain what to do.

"Gracious, Tim!" called Warren, as he came up, "that was the closest call you ever had."

"It's qu'ar," replied the other, "that after we had pumped about a ton of lead into him without hurting the spalpeen, he should dhrop down from a single shot."

"That's because it was aimed right."

"But ye had no bitter chance than meself, nor what ye also was given a few minutes ago."

"But it was not I, Tim, who fired the last shot."

"What are ye talking about?" demanded the other. "I had no chance to shoot me rifle, and who ilse could have done the same?"

"But I tell you I did not fire; I was about to do so, when someone else saved me the trouble; I am sure I couldn't have done any better than I did before."

"Thin who was the mon?"

The question naturally caused the couple to look around in quest of the unknown friend.

They saw him at the first glance.

"There he is! Look at him!" whispered Tim Brophy.

Less than a hundred yards away stood an Indian warrior, calmly watching them. He had mounted a bowlder, so that his figure was brought out in clear relief. He was in Indian costume, most of it being hidden by a heavy blanket gathered around the shoulders, but the leggings and moccasons showed beneath, and the head was ornamented with stained eagle-feathers. The noticeable fact about him, however, was that his black hair was short, and the feathers were fixed in a sort of band, which clasped the forehead. The rather pleasing face was fantastically daubed with paint, and he held a fine rifle in his right hand, the other being concealed under his blanket.

His action, or rather want of action, was striking. The bowlder which supported him was no more stationary than he. He gazed fixedly at the youths, but made no signs and uttered no word.

"Begorra, but he's a shtrange gintleman," muttered Tim. "I wonder if he's posin' for his picter."

"His firing of the gun proves that he is a friend," said Warren; "so we have nothing to fear from him."

"If that's the case why doesn't he come forward and interdooce himself? whisht now!"

What did the Irishman do but pucker up his mouth, whistle, and beckon to the Indian to approach. The latter, however, did not move a muscle.

"Helloa!" called Warren; "we thank you for your kindness; won't you come forward and join us?"

This appeal was as fruitless as the other.

"If the copper gintleman won't come to us I'm going to him."

It was just like Tim to start forward to carry out his intention, though a sense of delicacy restrained his companion from joining him. The Indian, however, nipped the little scheme in the bud.

The Irishman had taken only two or three steps, when the Sioux, as he evidently was, turned about, leaped lightly down from the bowlder, and vanished.

"Well, I'll be hanged!" exclaimed the disappointed Tim, stopping short; "ye may be a good rifle shot, but be the same token ye are not fond of selict company," and with a laugh he walked back to his friend, whose face was so grave as to attract the notice of the Irishman.

"What's the matter, Warren?"

"Do you know who that Indian is?"

"I niver have saan him before."

"Yes, you have, many a time; he's been at our house within the past few weeks."

"Who is he?"

"Starcus."

"Git out!"

"I'm not mistaken," insisted young Starr, compressing his lips and shaking his head. "He's painted and dressed like his people, but his short hair made me suspicious, and when he turned to jump down from the bowlder, he made a movement that fixed his identity beyond all doubt."

"Wal, ye're so sartin about it that I can't help belaving ye; but if it was Starcus, why did he act that way? Why didn't he spake, and why didn't he coom forward and shake hands wid us?"

"That's what troubles me; it wasn't like him. It makes me believe he has joined the hostiles."

"But if that is the case why did he interfere whin the grizzly was about to chaw me up?"

"His whole action was strange, but I explain it this way: He was prowling through this place, probably to help the bucks that are now on the warpath, when he heard our guns, made his way forward, and seeing the bear about to pounce upon you, he fired with the wish to save you. Your danger caused him to feel friendly toward us; for otherwise, instead of killing the bear he would have shot you and me."

"Maybe he fired at me instead of the bear," suggested Tim, "and it was a chance shot that saved meself."

"That cannot be, for he is too good a marksman to make such a miss. I have fired at a target with him and never saw a better shot than he. Then, too, when he found he missed, he could have turned his Winchester on us in turn and brought us both down."

"And ye think after his doing us that kindness, he became an inimy agin?"

"He has caught the craze that is setting his people wild, and though you didn't recognize him yesterday among that party of bucks near the house, I believe he was either there or was one of the horsemen that stampeded the cattle. He is with them body and soul. His last shot was given through impulse. Of course he knew us both, and acted from a generous motive. He may have stood there debating with himself whether to continue that friendship, when your advance scattered all his good resolutions to the winds. He has gone off to join the others, and when we meet again he will be our bitter foe, eager to serve us both as he served the grizzly. Let us not deceive ourselves about that."

45

"There's one thing that looks well," remarked Tim a moment later; "ifStarcus is wid the ither spalpeens, they haven't found your fayther and mither, for they're not in this part of the counthry."

"That gives me relief," said Warren, with a glowing face; "the folks must be many miles away, and these people are off their track altogether. Father will waste no time, but push on. This snow is not deep enough to bother them, and they ought to be safely within Fort Meade by nightfall."

"But what about us?" asked Tim significantly.

"This isn't our right latitude. We must pull out as quickly as we can. Our ponies are fresh, and can travel as fast as any of the Indian ones. We haven't far to go to reach the open country, and then we'll head for the fort, unless we conclude to hunt for the folks before reaching there. In the meantime, Tim, I'm hungry enough to eat my shoes."

"I'm wid ye there."

"We shall have to wait here long enough to cook a steak from that bear. He seems to be in fine condition, and will give us a good meal."

"There!" laughed the Irishman; "I knowed I had forgot something. Your mither give me a good, big lunch for us both whin I was laving yesterday, and it is in the residence beyant, onless yer pony ate up the same whin we warn't watching him."

"Little fear of that," replied the pleased Warren. "It is hardly the sort of food that he fancies. Come on; let's have a good meal, and then we'll be off."

CHAPTER IX.

ON THE BANK OF A STREAM.

It need not be said that George Starr wasted no time. Halting only long enough to say a few words to Tim Brophy before he set out to warn the son of his danger, he resumed his journey toward Fort Meade, some thirty miles away, at the base of the Black Hills.

He drew up beside the pony on which his wife sat with Dot in front. The pack-horse did not require leading, but as his load was lighter than either of the others, he kept his head at the haunch of the others, and plodded along as contentedly as they.

Though the route to the post by means of the regular trail was longer, it was always used when safe, because it was easy travelling throughout its whole extent. The country before the husband and wife was varied. There were miles of open plain, over which they could ride at a gallop, while in other places, the rocky ridges, broken timber, and gullies compelled detours that were likely to render a two days' journey necessary.

In addition to all this several streams must be crossed, and these were held in great dread, for if swimming became necessary, the plight of the little company, with the thermometer striking steadily below freezing point, would be pitiful indeed. The ranchman was resolved to save his wife and child from such an affliction, by constructing some kind of a raft, though the delay involved in such a work might solve the question of life and death.

"I have never been over this route—that is, to any extent," he remarked, after they had ridden a short time on a brisk walk; "I have followed the cattle for some miles among the hills yonder, but, as you know, we always used the regular trail when going to the fort."

"This is shorter," replied the wife, "because it is the most direct, and though there may be difficulties in the way, I am hopeful that we shall have no serious trouble."

"I hope so, too, but if I am not mistaken, we must cross more than one stream, and if they happen to be deep, it will be no trifling matter. How do you feel, Dot?" he asked, looking fondly at the little one, whose head was about the only portion visible beneath the folds of the blanket wrapped about her.

"I'm all right," replied the sweet voice, while the bright eyes twinkled happily, as though no thought of danger or sorrow had ever dimmed them.

"How long do you think you can ride on the back of Sally?"

"Just as long as she can carry me."

"That's good," laughed the parent, who could not help reaching across from the saddle and pinching the chubby cheek; "I want to give you a good long ride, and we may keep it up after dark."

"That don't make any difference to me, for I can sleep here as well as in my bed at home. Mamma will take care of me, won't you?" she asked, twisting her head about and looking up in the face of her parent.

The latter leaned down and kissed her, murmuring:

"Yes, with my life, precious one; but we are in the keeping of God, and he is always merciful and kind."

"I know that," said the child thoughtfully, "for hasn't He given me the best parents in the world? Oh, look! papa and mamma!" she added, forcing her head farther out of its environments, and pointing to the top of the elevation they were approaching.

The sight was a pretty one indeed. A noble buck had arrived first, from the other side of the ridge, and paused on the highest point. With his head erect, he looked down in wonderment at the party approaching him. He made a fine picture, with his antlers high in air and his whole form thrown in relief against the leaden sky beyond.

"What a fine mark," said the rancher admiringly; "I never saw a larger buck."

"You don't intend to shoot him?"

"No; we have all the food we are likely to want, and the sound of the gun might be dangerous to us, when there's no saying that other of the Sioux are not in the neighborhood."

"Isn't that too bad!"

The regretful exclamation of Dot was caused by the disappearance of the animal. The steady advance of the party was more than the timid creature could face. He whirled about and was off like a flash, to the keen regret of Dot, who was hoping for a closer acquaintance. The parents smiled at the innocence of the little one, and assured her it would have to be caught and tamed before allowing any companionship from anyone.

A few minutes later the friends rode to the top of the elevation, halting at the very spot where the buck had stood but a few minutes before.

"Just what I feared!" exclaimed the rancher regretfully.

As he spoke he pointed to the westward, where the gleam of water was seen, revealing a winding stream, which it was necessary to cross before continuing their journey.

"It is not broad and may not be deep," remarked the wife.

"That can be ascertained only by investigation."

He halted long enough to take a sweeping survey of the country behind them. There might have been Indians watching, but, if so, he detected no signs of them. The little party were conspicuous objects, but it was an easy matter for anyone to keep out of sight of the keenest vision on the crest of the elevation.

The stream that had caught his eye was about half a mile away, the intervening ground being a comparatively level and grassy plain, but beyond the water stretched a hilly and wooded section, which was likely to offer serious obstacles to their progress.

"We shall have snow before night," remarked Mr. Starr, glancing up and around at the sky, "and if it amounts to much it will make more trouble."

"Let us ride faster, then, while we may," said his wife, urging her pony into a gallop, which was instantly imitated by the other, though the gait was so distasteful to the pack-horse that he held back until sharply spoken to by his master. Finally all three struck a pace which speedily carried them to the stream that crossed their path.

It seemed odd that while there was plenty of timber on the other side, even to the water's edge, not a stick was on the bank where the fugitives halted. If it should be found necessary to make a raft with which to cross, Mr. Starr might well ask himself where the material was to be procured, since he saw none within reach.

The stream was less than a hundred yards wide and the current no' swift. The water was roiled to that extent that the bottom could be seen only a few paces from shore, but the slope was so gradual that the rancher was hopeful that the horse would be able to wade it.

He scanned the water and finally turned to his wife with a smile:

"Where do you think we had better try it, Molly?"

"I know of no way of learning the depth of water except by test," she replied; "if it were clearer, we could make use of our eyes."

"I wonder if it is clearer up yonder," he remarked, looking at a clump of bushes above them and some rods in extent. "It strikes me that it may be; anyway, I will find out."

Instead of riding to the spot he dismounted, and, rifle in hand, walked the short distance necessary. As he did so, naturally he gave more heed to the stream than to his footsteps, for it was the former in which his interest lay. Dot laughed merrily when he stumbled, and he looked about and shook his head in mock anger at her.

The bushes he approached were no more than three or four feet in height, not very dense, and continued with straggling interruptions as far as the eye could trace the winding stream.

Mrs. Starr, who was attentively watching her husband, saw him pause on reaching the stunted growth. He looked at the water and then at the bushes. Then he suddenly leaped back with an exclamation and came hastening to his wife, his white face and staring eyes showing that he had made a horrifying discovery.

CHAPTER X.

BENT ARM AND HIS BAND.

George Starr was so agitated that, forgetting the presence of his little child, he impulsively spoke the truth, while yet a few paces away:

"Plummer is in those bushes."

"Is he——"

Mrs. Starr hesitated with the dreadful word unuttered.

"Yes; he is dead; killed by the Indians!"

The wife gave a gasp, and the husband added:

"The poor fellow lies stretched out, stark and stiff, where he was shot down by the Sioux. He must have been killed shortly after leaving the house."

"Where is his horse?"

"I suppose it has been stolen. It is a sad thing, but poor Plummer is with his Maker; it won't do for us to wait any longer; I don't understand how we have escaped thus far, for we are in greater danger than I had supposed. We must cross the stream without delay, even if we have to swim our horses."

"I am ready," said Mrs. Starr calmly; "lead the way."

"I hope it will not be necessary to subject you and Dot to the trial, but there is not a minute to spare."

With his lips compressed, the rancher hastily remounted his pony and turned his head toward the water.

"Let me keep in advance," he said, "and you can tell what to do."

The obedient horse sniffed the water, but, without hesitation, stepped in, sinking to his knees within a yard of the bank.

A rod farther the depth had not materially increased, and, turning his head, he signified to his wife to follow. She clasped Dot a little closer to her breast, spoke quietly to her animal, and he obeyed without faltering.

The water steadily but slowly deepened, and when the middle of the stream was reached it was at the stirrups of the leader. He withdrew his feet and pushed on, the pony cautiously advancing, and the hope growing that the stream would be forded without trouble.

A rod farther, and Mrs. Starr uttered a slight exclamation. She saw the steed of her husband suddenly sink, and thought he was going entirely under. But he did not, and, by a quick raising of his feet, the rider saved them from wetting. His animal still retained a firm foothold, and, quickly recovering, kept forward.

Now the water began shallowing, and, with a relief beyond words, the rancher reached dry land without having suffered any inconvenience.

"Thank Heaven!" he exclaimed, turning about and watching his wife, who guided her animal over the invisible trail until she was beside him on the hard earth. It required no little skill on her part, for when she withdrew her foot from her stirrup, and was obliged not only to hold her own poise, but to take care of Dot, her task became delicate and difficult. But the little one behaved like a heroine. She did not speak or stir, through fear of disturbing her parent, and was as relieved as both when the current was safely forded.

"Are there any more like this?" asked the wife.

"There are other streams, but whether they can be forded or not remains to be learned."

The bank sloped upward to a height of a dozen feet, and beyond it declined nearly as much, and then stretched away in an open plain for more than a mile, before breaking into rough, rocky country, where they were quite sure to find greater obstructions confronting them than any yet encountered.

"Oh, see there!" called out Dot.

Flakes of scurrying snow were in the air, and her father supposed she referred to them.

"Yes," he replied, "we shall have to ride for a while through a snow storm."

"I know that, but it isn't what I mean; yonder is someone following us."

Her position in the arms of her mother gave her opportunity to look back over the stream they had just crossed, while the attention of her parents was directed elsewhere.

Her words caused both to glance behind them, where they witnessed a startling scene. A Sioux Indian, astride of a pony, had halted with the fore feet of the animal in the margin of the water. Directly behind him was a second horseman, advancing slowly, and immediately to the rear of him appeared a third, while the head and shoulders of a fourth were rising to view over the bank in the path of the others. And there was no saying how many others made up the procession, streaming toward the ford in the footsteps of the fugitives.

"Molly," said Mr. Starr, in a low voice, "ride over the top of the hill as quickly as you can."

"But what will you do?"

"Never mind; obey me at once or we are lost."

A HOT PURSUIT.

She obeyed without remonstrance, though her fear at that moment was more for her husband than for herself and child. She was quick-witted enough to jerk the reins sharply, so that her pony passed out of sight before the pursuers could suspect her purpose. But the moment she was behind the sheltering swell, she checked her horse and waited for her husband.

The latter decided on his course of action the moment the peril broke upon him.

He calmly confronted the advancing bucks and held himself ready to dispute their crossing. Unless he kept them in check and delayed the pursuit, nothing could save his family and himself.

The foremost Sioux evidently was the leader. Starr recognized him, despite his paint, as a fellow who had visited his home on several occasions, and who was known as Bent Arm, because of a peculiar rigidity of the left arm, made by some wound received years before.

While the white and red men sat on their ponies facing each other the remaining warriors continued coming into view until five of them were grouped behind the leader. There they sat—grim, silent, and watchful—leaving matters wholly in the hands of the one in front.

The latter, observing the rancher at bay, called to him in fair English:

"Wait dere—surrender—won't hurt."

"Why do you ask me to surrender? We are not enemies," called back the white man.

"Wait dere," repeated Bent Arm; "want to talk wid you."

"We are talking now; stay where you are, and let me hear what you have to say."

"We go over—we talk better dere."

It was plain that the Sioux was not satisfied with the action of the rancher's wife. She and her child were beyond sight, and it looked as if the parley of her husband was meant to give her a chance to get beyond reach. Valuable time was passing, and unless they acted promptly, they would throw away an opportunity that would never come to them again.

George Starr read their purpose as plainly as if they had announced it in so many words. Further talk was useless; the Sioux were bent on making him and his family prisoners, and little mercy would be shown them. He knew the dear ones were but a few paces away, and his wife would never leave the spot so long as he was in danger.

The words had hardly fallen from the lips of Bent Arm when his pony began stepping farther into the water, while his companions closed in behind him.

Striking his heels sharply against the sides of his horse as the rancher drew his head about, he sent the animal over the swell in a couple of bounds beyond reach of any shots that might be sent after him. He wondered a little that the Indians had not announced their presence by a volley that would have brought him from the saddle, but rightly judged the reason to be that they preferred to make the little party prisoners, considering them as good as already secured.

"Stay where you are!" he called to his wondering wife. "I am going to make a fight with them. Our only hope is in keeping them back until it is dark."

He was out of the saddle while speaking, and, dropping on his hands and knees, crawled up the swell and looked over.

CHAPTER XI.

AT BAY.

George Starr's pony, left to himself, wandered off to the side of the other one, on which sat Mrs. Starr, with Dot. The latter reached out her chubby hand and patted the silken nose of the intelligent horse, who liked the caress. The mother was too agitated to notice this by-play, but kept watch for her husband.

The latter crept to within a foot or two of the top of the swell, when he quickly but cautiously raised his head and peered over at the Sioux.

But a minute or two had passed since exchanging words with Bent Arm, but that brief period was improved as much by one party as the other. The Sioux leader's horse was in the stream to the depth of his knees, and the second Indian was in the act of entering, with the others close behind him.

It was no time for hesitation, for that meant death. Starr shoved his Winchester in front, so that the muzzle projected over the swell, took deliberate aim at Bent Arm, and let fly.

The distance was short, the rancher was an excellent marksman, and the bullet bored its way through the breast of the painted miscreant, who hardly knew what hurt him. With a screech, he threw up his arms, one grasping his gun, and toppled from the back of his pony, falling with a loud splash into the water, where for the moment he disappeared under the surface.

George Starr was never cooler in his life. He was fighting not only for his own existence, but for those who were dearer to him than that existence. He knew the mercilessness of the red men near at hand, and he was equally merciless to them.

This proceeding, as may be supposed, caused consternation for a moment among the advancing Sioux. The warrior immediately behind the leader stopped his pony abruptly, stared at the tuft of grass above which the faint puff of smoke was curling; and then, fearful of a second shot aimed at himself, whirled his animal about and sent him at one bound up the bank of the stream, where his companions, no less dismayed than he, threw themselves forward on the backs of their horses, to shield themselves from the aim of the rancher.

It was at this crisis that George Starr committed two blunders which threatened the very doom he was trying to escape. One of those errors, however, did credit to his heart, if not to his head.

Having opened the ball, he should have pushed things unmercifully. He was well aware of the venom of those red men, and, with his magazine rifle at command, he ought to have kept up an unremitting fire until he had tumbled several more to the ground, and driven the survivors beyond sight and the power of harm. It was his reluctance to perpetrate such slaughter, and the weak hope that he had already accomplished that result, that stayed his hand, at the moment when he should have steeled his feelings against sympathy. The other equally serious mistake was in staying where he was, prone on the ground, with a watchful eye on the marauders. He saw, when it was too late, that he should have dashed back to his pony, and leaped into the saddle and ridden with his wife, in all haste, for the refuge a mile away. Whether that would have proven a refuge or not was uncertain, but with the check given the Sioux he would have secured a start that promised everything.

Night was approaching, and, in the gathering gloom, it ought not to have been difficult, with the advantage named, to throw his pursuers off the trail. But he tarried until the chance was irrevocably gone.

The Sioux proved on more than one occasion, during their recent troubles in the West, that they were capable of daring, coolness, and heroism, and are quick to recover from a panic. When driven to bay they will fight like wild-cats, and the bleaching bones of many a brave soldier and officer bear eloquent witness to these qualities on their part.

Instead of breaking into a wild flight beyond the sheltering bank on the other side of the stream, as the rancher expected them to do, they held their places on the backs of their ponies, and, leaning over so as to protect themselves, returned the fire of the white man.

Looking across the narrow stream, they saw the slouch hat rising in the short grass, just behind the projecting muzzle of the Winchester, and a couple of them aimed and fired.

But the rancher was too alert to be caught in that fashion. The moment he observed the action of the red men, he dropped his head behind the swell of earth, and the bullets clipped the grass and scattered the dirt harmlessly within a few inches of his crown.

"Be careful!" called the anxious wife, who read the meaning of the flying soil; "they will hit you."

"Have no fear of me," replied the husband, without looking around; "I am all right; keep back where you are and hold yourself ready to ride as fast as you can when I give the word."

The rancher now did that which he should have done in the first place: he doffed his hat and laid it on the ground beside him. It was too conspicuous under the circumstances, and the Sioux were on the watch for it.

Waiting several minutes after the firing of the two shots, he stealthily raised his head high enough to look through the grass in front. An astonishing sight rewarded him.

In the brief interval that had passed after firing his rifle, the five Indians had dashed over the swell with their ponies where the latter were out of sight, and, flinging themselves on the ground, took precisely the same position as his own. They were now as safe from harm as himself. The duel was one of vigilance, caution, skill, and watchfulness, with the chances against the white man.

The keen gaze of the latter, wandering over the surface of the stream, detected a dark object some distance to the right, as it showed indistinctly on the surface, disappearing, and then slowly coming to view again farther down. He required no one to tell him that it was the victim of his marksmanship, drifting out of sight, as many a one had done before, when trying to stay the advancing tide of the hated Caucasian.

It struck the rancher that it would be well to let the Sioux know that he was still on guard. He caught glimpses here and there of the upper part of a repulsive face, with its long black hair and serpent-like eyes, on the alert to catch him unawares, and he fired at the nearest.

The aim was good, but there was no reason to believe that he had inflicted harm, though he must have come nigh it.

Strange it is that in the most trying moments, when it would seem that a trifling thought should be impossible on the part of a person, he sometimes gives way to a fancy that is of that nature. Recalling the story which he had read when a boy, and which is familiar to all our readers, the rancher now picked up his hat at his side and gently raised it to view, taking care to lower his own head beyond reach of harm.

Instantly a couple of rifles cracked from the other side of the stream, and he smiled grimly when he saw the marks of the bullets in the crown.

"They shoot well," he said, turning his face toward his wife and holding up the hat, "but they made a slight mistake that time."

If the Sioux supposed that the last shots were fatal, they were likely to repeat their attempt to cross. That would never do, and, more with a view of letting them know no harm had resulted, than in the hope of inflicting injury, the rancher took aim at what seemed to be the forehead of one of the warriors, a short distance up stream, and fired.

To his amazement, the wild screech left no doubt that the shot was fatal. The bullet had bored its way through the bronzed skull of the miscreant, and the force of assaulting Sioux was now reduced by one-third.

CHAPTER XII.

FACING WESTWARD.

The rancher was astonished beyond measure at the success of his shot. He had looked for nothing of the kind, but there could be no mistake as to the result; there was nothing to be gained by any pretence on the part of the Sioux. He certainly was as dead as dead could be.

How he longed, like a certain famous general, for the coming of night! A little more darkness and he would flee with his wife and child under its friendly cover, and place a safe distance between them and their enemies, before the latter could learn of their flight.

Several minutes passed without a demonstration on either side, but while matters stood thus, a new danger presented itself to the rancher. Why should the Sioux stay where they were? What was to prevent them moving farther up or down the bank, under the screen it afforded, and crossing unobserved? The winding course of the current gave every chance of doing this, and surely they were not likely to forget such an obvious course.

The thought had hardly presented itself to the watcher when that very thing was attempted. The one who essayed it, however, forgot the caution he should have remembered.

The slowly settling night and the falling snow may have misled him, but when the warrior rode his pony into the stream at a point considerably above, Starr observed him at the moment he began descending the bank.

This was something that must be nipped in the bud. He shifted his position to where the grass gave slightly better protection, and sighted with the utmost care and deliberation.

The shot was successful, but not precisely as he counted upon. The bullet, instead of striking the rider, pierced the brain of the pony, who reared frantically, plunged forward on his knees, and rolled upon his side, the Sioux dexterously saving himself by leaping away and scurrying behind the swell before the white man could fire a second time.

"If they try it at that point, they will do so at some other," was the conclusion of the rancher, turning his gaze down stream. But the current made such a sharp bend near at hand, that his view was shortened, and the effort could be successfully made without detection on his part.

An unexpected diversion occurred at this moment. The pack-horse, that had been contentedly cropping the grass near at hand and paying no heed to what was going on about him, wandered toward the bank, and was in imminent peril of being shot by the vigilant Sioux before he could be turned away.

Mrs. Starr called sharply to him, and her voice caused the prostrate husband to look around. The pony at that moment was ascending the swell, to go down on the other side to the water, where he would have been in plain sight of the red men.

Fearful that words would not check him, the rancher sprang up and, bending his head to save himself from his foes, ran the few steps necessary to reach the animal. Catching hold of his bridle, he jerked his head in the opposite direction, and, to teach him prudence, delivered a vigorous kick. The startled animal headed toward the west and broke into a gallop straight across the plain.

"Let him go," said the impatient owner, looking after him: "he is too lazy to travel far, and we'll follow him soon."

"Why not do so now?" asked his wife.

"I fear that they are looking for such a move, and will be across before we can gain sufficient start."

"But they may do so now."

"Am I not watching them?" asked the husband, beginning to creep up the swell again, but pausing before he was high enough to discern the other side.

"They may cross above or below, where you cannot see them," remarked the wife, giving utterance to the very fear that had troubled him some minutes before.

"They may do so, but I have just defeated such an attempt, and they will probably wait a while before repeating it."

"Then we can have no more favorable time to leave them than now."

"Such would be the fact, if I only knew of a surety that they would wait a while."

"I am afraid you are making a mistake, George."

"It may be, but my judgment is against what you propose. Suppose that, at the moment of starting, they should appear on this side; they would run us down within a few hundred yards."

"Are not our ponies as fleet as theirs?"

"Probably; but with Dot to look after, you would have more than your hands full, and nothing could save us."

"I could manage her very well; but do as you think best. We can only pray to Heaven to protect us all."

Looking to the westward, the rancher saw the pack-pony just vanishing from sight in the gloom. Brief as was the time that he had left the Sioux without watching, he felt that it had been too long, and he now made his way up the swell until he could peer over at the other bank, where the red men were awaiting the very chance he gave them that moment.

The narrowest escape of his life followed. Providentially, his first glance was directed at the precise spot where a crouching Sioux made a slight movement with his rifle, which gave the white man an instant's warning of his peril. He ducked his head, and had he not instinctively closed his eyes, would have been blinded by the dust and snow thrown against his face, as the leaden ball whizzed through the air, falling on the prairie a long distance away.

In its flight it passed directly over the heads of the wife and child, who noticed the peculiar whistling sound a few feet above them. But they were as safe from such danger as if a mile away. The swell of the bank would not allow any missile to come nigh enough to harm them.

"Don't be frightened," he said, with a reassuring smile, "they can't touch you as long as they are on the other side."

"But how long will they stay there?" asked the wife, unable to repress her uneasiness over the tardiness of her husband.

"Molly," said he, stirred by a sudden thought, "why not ride after the pack-horse?"

"And leave you here?" was the astonished question.

"Only for a few minutes; you will gain a good start, and it won't take me long to come up with you. I can put my pony on a run, and we shall gain invaluable time."

But this was asking more than the obedient wife was willing to grant. No possible circumstances could justify her in deserting her husband. If he fell, she had no wish to escape.

Dot, who had held her peace so long, now spoke:

"Papa, don't ask us to leave you, 'cause we don't want to. I asked mamma to let me go to you, but she says no."

Tears filled the eyes of the father, and his voice trembled as he said:

"Very well, little one; stay with your mamma, and when the time comes for us to start we will go together."

"But why don't you go now?" persisted the child, taking her cue, perhaps, from the words her mother had spoken.

"I will not keep you waiting long," he assured her, more affected by the question of the child than by the arguments of her mother.

Shifting the point of observation, the rancher raised his head just enough, cautiously parting the grass in front, to permit him to see the other bank, becoming more dimly visible in the falling snow and gathering gloom.

He scanned the points whence had come the shots, but could discover nothing of his enemies. They might be there, but if so they were invisible, as could readily be the case; but, somehow or other, the conviction grew upon him that they were moving, and that to postpone his departure longer was to invite the worst fate imaginable for himself and dear ones.

"We cannot leave too soon," he exclaimed, hastening to carry out the purpose that never ought to have been delayed so long.

CHAPTER XIII.

IN THE FRINGE OF THE WOODS.

Fully realizing the mistake he had made in waiting, the rancher now did his best to improve the precious time at his disposal.

His own pony had remained obediently near his companion, while the brush was going on between his master and the Sioux on the other side of the stream. The former hastily climbed into the saddle, and taking the reins in hand, looked at his wife.

"Are you ready, Molly?"

"I have been for a long time."

"Come on; keep close to me."

He spoke briskly to his horse, who broke into a swift gallop, which was imitated so promptly by the other that the couple advanced abreast toward the wooded section. It was no time for conversation, and the progress continued in silence.

The snow was now falling thick and fast, and the gloom had deepened to that extent that they could not see objects more than a hundred feet away. Both wife and husband continually glanced behind them, for they were almost certain that the red men were in the act of crossing the stream at the moment the start was made, and could not be far to the rear.

True, the fugitives had much in their favor. The keen eyes of the pursuers could detect their trail in the snowy ground, but not for long. By and by they might trace it only by dropping down from their ponies and using the sense of feeling. This would compel them to proceed carefully, and hold them well to the rear while the whites were using the occasion to the utmost, and continually gaining ground. Had the route to Fort Meade been level and unobstructed, they could have asked nothing more favorable. They would have forced their ponies to the utmost, and by the time the sun rose the vengeful red men would be placed hopelessly behind.

The straining vision saw nothing but the darkness and snow in the direction of the stream already crossed, but they could never feel relieved of the dreadful fear until safely within the military post of the Black Hills.

"Oh, papa, I see a horse!" was the startling exclamation of Dot, whom her mother had supposed, because of her stillness and immobility, to be asleep.

"Where?" demanded her father, grasping his Winchester and looking affrightedly around.

"Not there," replied the child with a laugh, working her arm out of its environments, and pointing ahead.

A solitary animal was observed standing as motionless as a statue a short distance in advance. Apprehensive of some trap by the Indians, the father brought his pony to a sudden stop, his wife instantly imitating him, and both peered ahead at the strange form.

They could see no rider, though there was something on the animal's back, which might have been a warrior lying flat, so as to protect his body from the rifle of the white man, or, what was equally probable, the owner was standing on the ground hidden by the horse, and awaiting his chance to send in a fatal shot.

"What's the matter?" asked Dot, puzzled by the action of her parents.

"S-h! We are afraid a bad Indian is there."

"Why, can't you see that's Jerry?"

Jerry was the name of the pack pony.

"Of course it is. Why didn't we think of it?" asked the father the next moment, relieved beyond measure by the discovery.

Jerry seemed to be of the opinion that it was the place of his friends to make the advances, for he did not stir until they rode up beside him.

The lazy fellow was found with his load intact. He had been given all the time he could ask for his journey to this point, and evidently was a little sulky over the treatment received at the hands, or rather the foot, of his master, for his head had to be jerked several times before he faced about, and then it required more vigorous treatment to force him into a lazy gallop.

Luckily, the greater part of the plain had been crossed before this reunion took place, and the party had not gone far when the rancher allowed the animals to drop to a walk. In front loomed a dark mass, which he recognized as the fringe of the wood observed from the bank of the stream behind them. Through this it was necessary to thread their way with extreme care, owing to the darkness and their unfamiliarity with the ground.

Upon reaching the edge of the wood the fugitives came to a stand-still.

Slipping from his saddle, the rancher brushed away the snow at his feet and pressed his ear against the ground.

"I can hear nothing of them," he remarked, resuming the upright posture; "I am quite hopeful that that party will molest us no more."

"It won't do to count on it," were the wise words of his wife.

"I think you had better dismount and lead your pony," said the rancher; "we can mount again when through the wood; there will be less danger from the trees and limbs, and you and Dot must be cramped from sitting so long."

He helped them to the ground. It was a relief indeed to both, for they had kept their places on the back of the horse for a number of hours. Dot yawned, stretched her limbs, and felt as though nothing would delight her so much as a frolic in the snow. The thoughtful mother had provided her not only with thick, strong shoes, but with heavy stockings, leggings, and warm clothing, with which she was well protected against the storm that was impending when they left their home.

Nothing could have better shown the childish innocence of her nature than her action in slyly removing her mittens, stooping down, packing a wad of snow with her hands and flinging it against her father's face, with a merry laugh.

"Gracious, Dot! how you startled me!" he said, looking around at her.

"Did I hurt you?"

"No; but don't speak or laugh so loud, for some of the bad Indians may be near."

"I forgot about that, but I'm going to hit Jerry, for he is so lazy he needs it."

And the indolent animal received a tiny whack from the snowy missile projected by the chubby hand of the child. He seemed to think, however, that it was no more than a snowflake, for he did not give even an extra wink of the eye.

The delay was only momentary, when the rancher, with one hand grasping the bridle-rein and the other parting the limbs and bushes in front, began groping his way through the growth of timber, where it was so dark that everyone's eyes were practically useless.

Directly behind the horse walked Dot, with her mother next, leading her pony, and the pack-horse bringing up the rear.

Ten minutes of this cautious progress and the leader checked himself with an impatient expression.

"What is it?" called the wife, in a guarded voice.

"Another stream of water."

"Do you know anything about it?"

"Nothing; I came near tumbling into it, with Dick on top of me; if he hadn't scented it first I would have done so."

"What is to be done?" asked Mrs. Starr, as grievously disappointed as her husband.

"I'm blessed if I know; it may be half a mile deep and ten miles across, with a perpendicular bluff a thousand feet high on the other side."

Leaving her pony, the wife took the hand of Dot and joined him where he had halted on the edge of the unknown stream.

"I've made up my mind that we shall do one thing right away," he remarked decisively.

"What's that?"

"Eat supper while we have the chance; Jerry is on hand with the provisions, and he may be somewhere else in the morning."

"I'm glad of that," said the happy Dot, "for I'm awfuller hungry than I ever was in all my life."

"Then supper it is."

CHAPTER XIV.

TURNED BACK.

It was a wise proceeding on the part of the rancher. The opportunity to make a substantial repast was theirs, and as he had remarked, there was no certainty when it would come again.

The bag in which the provisions were placed was taken from the back of Jerry, and the father helped his child and wife, who ate until they were fully satisfied. He dipped up water with Dot's small tin cup from the stream in front, and with it their thirst was slaked.

"Molly," he suggested, "you can carry one or two of the sandwiches without inconvenience."

"Yes."

"Let us both do so; we may lose Jerry, and if so, they will come in handy."

"I have a couple, too," said Dot.

"It isn't best that you should burden yourself with them."

"But I can't help it, papa."

"How is that?"

"They're inside of me," and the parents, even in their great dread, smiled at the odd conceit of the little one, who chuckled softly to think how she had "fooled" her papa.

The delay was brief. The rancher knew that it was impossible to reach Fort Meade without crossing the stream before them, with the probability that still others awaited them at no great distance. It can be understood with what depth of dread he contemplated swimming the animals over, with the certainty of the saturation of all their garments, on this winter night, and the cold steadily increasing.

In short, it meant perishing, unless a fire was kindled, in which case, a delay would be necessitated that would throw away all the advantage secured by flight. He was determined not to do it, unless actually driven to it as a last resource.

He did not forget that he was now where there was an abundance of material with which a raft could be constructed that would obviate this exposure, but the building of such a rude craft, under the circumstances, was next to impossible. He had no implement except his pocket knife, and might grope about in the darkness for hours without getting together enough timber to float them to the other side.

Obviously one of two things must be done—try to cross where they were or follow the bank down until a fording place could be found, and repeated trials were likely to be necessary before success was obtainable.

Singular it is that so often out of the mouths of babes are heard the words of wisdom.

The rancher had risen to his feet, and was in the act of mounting his pony to enter the water, when Dot spoke:

"Why don't you let Dick go ahead and you ride behind on Sally?"

"Well, I declare!" exclaimed the father admiringly; "I begin to believe that if we reach the fort, it will be through your guidance, my precious little one," and, stooping over, he kissed her cheek.

"Strange that we did not think of that," remarked the mother. "Dot is wise beyond her years."

The plan was adopted at once.

The mare ridden by the mother and child, and the horse of the father, were so intelligent that no risk was involved in the essay, which insured against the immersion held in such natural dread.

The saddle and trappings were removed from Dick, while the rancher mounted upon the side-saddle belonging to his wife. Then the horse was ordered to enter the water, and, with some hesitation, he obeyed, his owner being but a step or two behind on the mare.

The gloom was so deep that the hearing, and not the sight, must be depended upon. That, however, was reliable when nothing was likely to occur to divert it from its duty.

The stream was no more than fairly entered when the rancher made two unwelcome discoveries: The current was much stronger than he had anticipated, and the water deepened rapidly. Ten feet from shore it touched the body of the mare.

Inasmuch, however, as Dick was still walking, there was hope that the depth might increase no more, or, at most, not to a dangerous extent.

Mr. Starr could not see his own horse, but he plainly heard him as he advanced cautiously, feeling his way, and showing by his sniffing that the task was anything but pleasant to him. Not knowing the width of the stream, it was impossible to tell in what portion of it they were: but he was already listening for the sounds which would show that his animal was climbing out on the other side, when the very thing he feared took place.

A loud splash, followed by a peculiar rustling noise, showed that Dick was swimming.

At the same moment the mare sank so deeply that, had not the rider thrown his feet backward along her spine, with his body extended over the saddle and her neck, he would have been saturated to the knees. As it was, Sally was within a hair of being carried off her feet by the force of the current.

The rancher drew her head around, and, after a sharp struggle, she held her own, and began laboring back to the shore she had left; putting forth such vigor that it was plain the task was far more agreeable than the one upon which she first ventured.

Meanwhile, Dick was swimming powerfully for the farther bank, and before his owner could think of calling to him, owing to his own flurry, he heard his hoofs stamp the hard earth. True, he had landed, but that brief space of deep water was as bad as if its width were ten times as great; it could not be passed without the saturation of the garments of all, and that, as has been said, was not to be endured.

Before the mare could return Mr. Starr called to his pony, and the animal promptly obeyed, emerging only a minute after the mare from the point where he had entered.

"It's no use," he said to his waiting wife and little one; "there is one place where the horses must swim."

"Did you get wet, papa?" enquired Dot, solicitous for his welfare.

"No; but I came mighty near it."

"Then I suppose we must follow down the stream, and try it elsewhere," said the wife.

"Yes, with the discouraging fact that we are likely to pass a dozen fordable points, and strike a place that is deeper than anywhere else."

The saddles were readjusted, and the move made without delay. Since it was hard to thread their way through the wood, which lined the stream only a short distance from the water, they withdrew from it to the prairie, where travelling was easier.

Reaching the open plain, but keeping close to the margin of the timber, from which, fortunately, they had emerged at a point considerably removed from that of the entrance, the rancher repeated the precaution he had used before.

"Wait a moment," he said, in a low voice.

Once more the snow was brushed aside at his feet and the ear pressed against the ground.

To his dismay he heard the tramp of horses' hoofs on the hard earth.

"They are near at hand!" he said, in a startled whisper; "we must get away as quickly as we can."

He hastily helped his wife and little one on the back of the mare, mounted his own animal, and, with the pack-horse at the rear, moved along the timber on a rapid walk, continually peering off in the gloom, as though it was possible for him to see the Sioux, who certainly were at no great distance.

One fear troubled him: Suppose they should resort to the same artifice as he, and one of them appeal to the earth for evidence. He would be equally quick to discover the proximity of the fugitives, and with his sense of hearing trained to the finest point by many years' exercise, would locate the whites with unerring precision.

CHAPTER XV.

MISSING.

But there was no avoiding the risk. In silence the little party threaded their way along the margin of the prairie, listening for the sounds they dreaded to hear, and peering through the gloom for the forms they held in unspeakable fear. Not until they had progressed several hundred yards can it be said that the rancher breathed freely. Then he checked his pony, and those behind him did the same.

The next instant he was out of the saddle, with his ear once more against the cold earth.

Not the slightest sound reached him through this better conductor. If the Sioux horsemen were moving, they were too far off for the fact to be known. When first heard, they must have been close to the wood, on reaching which they undoubtedly dismounted and advanced on foot.

In that event, they must detect the footprints of the ponies in advance, and with their skill in trailing were certain to learn of the course taken by the whites. Then the pursuit would be resumed in earnest, and the perils would increase.

One possible remedy suggested itself, though there was no certainty of its success. The snow was now falling so fast that it promised to obliterate the footprints to that extent that they could not be followed in the dark. As it was, even the lynx eyes of the Sioux could avail them nothing. One of their number must be continually dismounting and using his hands to make sure they were not off the track. A half hour or more interval, and this resource would be taken from them by the descending snow.

It was this belief which caused the rancher to ride Dick among the trees, where he and the rest dismounted. Then they groped forward with no little difficulty for some rods and halted.

"Be careful," he said, speaking particularly to Dot, "and do not make any noise, for I believe those bad Indians are not far off, and they are looking for us."

Dot showed her obedience by not venturing to whisper.

It was not Mr. Starr's purpose to lose time by staying where they were. Accordingly, after threading their way for some distance farther, he emerged once more on the plain, and, as they remounted, rode straight away from the timber.

The object of this stratagem can be readily understood. The pursuing Sioux, after discovering that the trail of the fugitives led along the margin of the wood, were likely to override it for some way, before learning the fact. Then they would turn about and hunt until they found it again. The fact that at that point it entered the timber must cause another delay, where the difficulty of tracing the whites would be greatly increased. By the time they came back again to the open plain, the fall of snow was likely to render further pursuit almost, if not quite, impossible.

This was the theory which guided the rancher's actions, though he was too wise to lose sight of the probability of serious miscalculations on his part. There was another danger, however, of which he failed to think, but which was not long in manifesting itself.

By shifting his course so often, and leaving the stream altogether, he was sure to lose his bearings in the darkness. Instead of following the most direct route to Fort Meade, he was liable to turn back on his old trail, with the result that when the sun rose in the morning he would be in the vicinity of his home, with the environing perils more threatening than ever.

Beyond all question this would have been the result had not nature come to his help. He was on the point of turning his pony's head around, to re-enter the timber he had left, when he discovered to his astonishment that he had already reached it. There were the trees directly in front, with the nose of Dick almost touching a projecting limb.

He was at a loss to understand it until his wife suggested that the winding course of the stream was responsible for the situation. Even then he hardly believed until investigation convinced him that it was the same swift current flowing in front.

"We unconsciously strayed from a direct course, and must have been going at right angles to the correct one."

"There is no saying, George; only I advise you not to make too many experiments in the darkness. Several hours have passed since night came, and we are not making much progress toward the fort."

"You are quite right," was the nervous response, "but safety seemed to demand it. How are you standing it, Dot?"

The child made no answer.

"She is asleep," whispered the mother.

"I hope that it may last until morning. If you are tired of holding her in your arms I will take her."

"When I grow weary of that," was the significant reply of the wife, "I will let you know."

Inasmuch as the continually obtruding stream must be crossed, and the precious hours were fast passing, the rancher gave every energy to surmounting the difficulty.

As he led the way once more to the edge of the water, he asked himself whether the wisest course was not to construct a raft. The work promised to be so difficult, however, that he would have abandoned the thought had he not come upon a heavy log, lying half submerged at the very spot where he struck the water.

"This will be of great help," he said to his wife.

Leaning his Winchester against the nearest tree, he drew out his rubber safe and struck a match. The appearance of the log was encouraging, and after some lifting and tugging he succeeded in rolling it into the stream.

That ended the matter. To his chagrin, the water-soaked wood sank like so much mud.

"We won't experiment any longer," concluded the disappointed rancher; "but try the same thing as before."

Dick was stripped again and put in the lead, with his master following on the back of the mare. Mrs. Starr, being helped to the ground, stood with the sleeping Dot in her arms, awaiting the return of her husband from his disagreeable experiment.

"Heaven grant that this maybe the right place," was his prayer, as he entered upon the second essay; "if we are turned back again I shall be in despair."

His interest was intensified, for he was impressed with the belief that this was to be the decisive and final test.

As if Dick, too, felt the seriousness of the situation, he stepped resolutely forward, bracing himself against the strong current which was heard washing about his limbs. It seemed to the anxious rancher that he could discern the figure of his pony as he led the way through the gloom, only a short distance in advance of the mare.

When certain that they were fully half-way across, his heart began to beat with hope at finding that the water did not touch the stirrup in which one foot rested. It was plain also that the leading horse was still firmly wading.

With a relief which possibly may be imagined, the horseman heard Dick step out on the bank a few minutes later. He had waded the whole distance, thus proving that the stream was easily fordable at that point.

The delighted rancher could hardly repress a cheer. But for his fear that the Sioux might be in the vicinity, he would have announced the joyous fact to his wife.

"Perhaps, however, her sharp ears have told her the truth," was his thought, as he wheeled the mare about and started to return, leaving Dick to follow him, as he would be needed to help the party over.

With never a thought of danger, the animal was forced hastily through the water, coming out a few paces below where she had entered it.

"We are all right," he called; "we will be over in a jiffy."

To his astonishment there was no response. He pronounced his wife's name, but still no reply came. Then he moved up and down the bank, stirred by an awful fear, but heard and found her not.

CHAPTER XVI.

A THIEF OF THE NIGHT.

When the rancher entered the current with the two ponies, the interest of the wife, who remained behind with little Dot, was centred wholly in his effort to ford the stream. She stood on the very margin of the water, where, though unable to see the form of the rider or either of the animals, she could hear the sound made by them in passing through the current.

In this position, the pack-pony remained a few steps behind her and about half-way to the open plain. The child, who had been somewhat disturbed by the shifting about of herself, had fallen asleep again and rested motionless in her arms, with her form nestling in the protecting blanket.

Everything was silent except the slight noise caused by the animals in the water. In this position, with her nerves strung to the highest point, and her faculties absorbed in the single one of hearing, she caught a suspicious sound immediately behind her. It was as if Jerry was moving from the spot where he had been left.

Fearful of his going astray, her lips parted to speak, when, fortunately, she held her peace. It might be that some person was the cause of his action.

With the purpose of learning the truth, she stole through the timber toward the spot where he was standing a few minutes before. She was so close behind him, and moved so much faster, that she reached the open plain almost on his heels. Despite the gloom, she could make out his figure; and her feelings may be imagined when she distinguished the form of a Sioux warrior leading him.

Not only that, but the thief paused as soon as the open prairie was reached and lightly vaulted upon his back, beside the load already resting there. Then he hammered his heels against his ribs and the lazy beast rose to a jogging trot, immediately disappearing in the snow and darkness.

The wife, as may be supposed, was dumfounded and uncertain what to do, if indeed she could do anything. At the moment when it looked as if all danger was past, one of their enemies had unexpectedly stolen their pack-pony.

Where were the rest? Why did they content themselves with this simple act, when they might have done a thousandfold worse? How soon would the rest be on the spot? Was there no hope now of escape for the miserable fugitives?

These and similar thoughts were passing through her mind, when she heard her husband calling to her in a cautious voice. Not daring to reply, through fear of attracting the attention of their enemies, she threaded her way through the timber, and reached his side at the moment his heart was filled with despair at the belief that something frightful had taken place.

The joy of the rancher, on clasping his beloved wife once more in his arms, caused him to forget everything else for the moment, but she quickly made known the startling incident that had occurred.

"Heavens!" he muttered, "they have traced us after all, but where are the rest?"

"They must be near," she replied, laying her hand on his arm. "Listen!"

They did so, but heard nothing more.

"We must cross at once," he whispered.

No time was lost in following the prudent suggestion. The wife was helped upon the back of the mare, Dot still remaining asleep, and the husband, mounted on Dick, placed himself in front.

"There is only one place, and that lasts but for a few steps, where you will have to raise your foot to protect it from the water," he said, as they were about to enter the stream.

"I will remember," she nervously replied; "don't wait."

Once again the faithful pony entered the water, the mare so close behind that husband and wife could have touched each other, and the fording of the current began.

The rancher did not forget that it was impossible in the darkness to follow precisely his own course. Having emerged at a different point from where he entered, he was in reality following a different course, which might be the same as if it were a half mile farther up or down stream.

This proved to be the case, though the disappointment was of an agreeable nature, for the ponies struck a shallower part than that which was first forded. At no portion did the water do more than barely touch the bodies of the animals, and then only for a few steps. Once the mare slipped on a smooth stone, and came within a hair of unseating her rider, but the latter's skill enabled her to retain her seat, and a few minutes later the two came out on the other side, without a drop of moisture on their garments.

"Thank Heaven!" was the fervent ejaculation of the husband as the fact was accomplished. "It is better than I expected."

"But don't forget that they may have done the same thing, and perhaps are awaiting us near at hand."

"You may be right, Molly, and we cannot be too careful."

The words were barely uttered when the splashing of water behind them left no doubt that the Sioux were again on their trail.

"Quick!" whispered the husband; "dismount; you can't ride the mare among the trees; she will follow, and don't fail to keep close behind Dick."

It was important, above all things, to leave the spot before the red men landed. Otherwise, they would hear the horses and locate them without difficulty.

A disappointment awaited our friends. It will be remembered that the fringe of timber on the other side was quite narrow, and they naturally supposed it corresponded on the farther shore. But after threading their way for double the distance, they were surprised to find no evidence of the open plain beyond.

The rancher dared not continue farther while there was reason to fear their pursuers were near. The brushing of the branches against the bodies of the animals and the noise of their hoofs could be detected in the silence, and was sure to betray the fugitives to any Sioux within a hundred yards.

The wife understood why the halt was made. Her husband stole back and placed himself by her side.

"You must be wearied with carrying Dot so long," he said sympathizingly.

"It is quite a trial," she replied, in the same guarded voice, "but there is no help for it, and I beg you to give the matter no thought."

"Let me take her a while."

"No, that will not do; you must hold your gun ready for instant use, and you could not do so with her in your arms. It is not so hard when we are sitting on the mare, for it is easy to arrange it so that she supports most of her weight."

"You are a good, brave woman, Molly, and deserve to be saved."

"Sh!" she admonished; "I hear something."

He knew she was right, for he caught the sound at the same moment. Someone was stealing through the wood near them. It was a person, beyond question, for a horse would have made more noise, and the sounds of his hoofs would have been more distinct than anything else. That which, fell upon their ears was the occasional crackling of a twig, and the brushing aside of the obtruding limbs. No matter with what care an Indian warrior threaded his way through the timber in this dense gloom, he could not avoid such slight evidences of his movements—so slight, indeed, that but for the oppressive stillness and the strained hearing of the husband and wife they would not have detected them.

Confident that the red man could not trace them in the gloom, even though so dangerously near, the dread now was that the ponies would betray them. Those watchful animals often prove the most valuable allies of the fleeing fugitive, for they possess the power of discovering impending danger before it can become known to their masters. But when they make such discovery they are apt to announce it by a stamp of the hoof or with a sniffing of the nostrils, which, while serving the master well, has the disadvantage also of apprising the enemy that his approach has become known.

Stealing from his position beside his wife, the rancher stepped to the mare and passed his hand reassuringly over her mouth, doing the same with his own pony. This action was meant as a command for them to hold their peace, though whether it was understood to the extent that it would be obeyed, remains to be seen.

CHAPTER XVII.

THROUGH THE WOOD.

Even in that trying moment, Starr could not help reflecting upon the peculiar turn matters had taken. He failed to understand the action of the solitary Sioux on the other side, who had contented himself with the simple theft of the pack-pony, when he might have done tenfold more injury to the fugitives.

And now, judging from the slight sounds that reached him, there was another single warrior prowling through the wood, instead of several. It might be, however, that his companions were near, awaiting the result of his reconnoissance, and would descend upon the whites the instant the way opened.

But these speculations were cut short by the alarming discovery that some strange fatality was bringing the scout fearfully close to where the husband and wife were standing beside their animals, hardly daring to speak in the most guarded whispers.

It must have been that the ponies understood what was expected from them, for they gave not the least sound. There was not a stamp of a hoof, and their breathing was as gentle as an infant's. So long as they remained mute it would seem that the peril must pass by.

And so it ought to have done, for assuredly the Indian could have gained no clew to the whereabouts of the fugitives from them or their animals.

But all the same, George Starr was not long in making the uncomfortable discovery that the red man was at his elbow, and the crisis was upon him.

The rancher knew where the miscreant was, and he determined to chance it. He silently clubbed his Winchester, brought it back over his left shoulder, and, concentrating his utmost strength in his arms, brought down the butt of this weapon with resistless force.

It could not have been better aimed had the sun been shining. It crashed on the crown of the unsuspecting Sioux, who sank silently to the earth, and it is enough to say that the "subsequent proceedings interested him no more."

"Sh!" whispered the husband; "there may be others near us; do you hear anything?"

Neither could catch any suspicious noise, and he concluded it was best to move on. If they should remain where they were when daylight came, all hope would be gone. The situation would be hardly improved if they stayed any longer in the gloom, after what had taken place.

Making known his purpose to his wife, he placed himself at the head of Dick, and holding his bit, started forward. The mare followed the moment she heard what was going on, and the mother with her child walked between.

But less than twenty steps were taken, when the leader paused abruptly, alarmed by an altogether unexpected discovery. The twinkle of a light appeared among the trees in front, so directly in their path that, had they continued straight forward, they would have stepped into the blaze.

This was cause for astonishment, and suggested that the fugitives had struck a place where other Sioux had gathered, probably a number who knew nothing of what had taken place a short time before. If this were true, there ought not to be much difficulty in working past them.

Still, critical as was the situation, he felt that the chance to learn something ought not to be thrown away. Whispering to his wife to remain where she was, he left her and stole forward until he could gain sight of the blaze and those surrounding it.

There was the fire made by a number of sticks heaped against the trunk of a tree, and burning vigorously, but to his surprise, not an Indian was in sight. How many had been gathered there, how long since they had left, whether they would return, and if so, how soon? All these were questions that must be left to some other time before even attempting to guess the answers.

He waited some minutes, thinking possibly the missing warriors would return, but not one showed up, and he felt it would not do to tarry longer. A goodly portion of the night had already passed, and Fort Meade was still a long distance away, with a dangerous stretch of country to pass.

It seemed to the husband and wife that they hardly breathed, as they moved through the wood. He held his pony by the rein with his left hand, while he used the right, grasping the Winchester, to open the way in front. They could do nothing more, listening meanwhile for the sounds of danger which they expected to hear every moment.

But lo! while they were advancing in this guarded manner, they suddenly came out of the wood and into the open country again.

The husband uttered another exclamation of thankfulness, and checked the animals.

"Now it looks as if we had a chance to accomplish something," he said, "and I am sure you are in need of rest."

"I am somewhat weary, but I can stand a great deal more, George; give no thought to me, but think only of the peril from which we must escape this night or never."

He gently took the little Dot, swathed as she was in the heavy blanket, and held her while his wife remounted the mare, without help. We have said she was an excellent horsewoman, as she had proved before this eventful night.

"Now," said he, when she was firmly seated and extended her arms to take the child, "I am going to use my authority as a husband over you."

"Have I not always been an obedient wife?" she asked, with mock humility.

"No man was ever blessed with a better helpmate," was the reply.

"I await your commands, my lord."

Instead of passing the child to her, he reached up his rifle.

"What is the meaning of that?" she asked wonderingly.

"Lay it across the saddle in front, where its weight will not discommode you. I shall carry Dot."

"But think, George, of the risk it involves. I assure you that it will be no task for me to take care of her now that I am in the saddle again."

"All discussion is ended," he replied, with a severity which she well knew was assumed, though she did not dispute him. She accepted the weapon and placed it in position as he directed. Then supporting the precious child with one arm, he mounted his pony and placed himself by her side.

"We will ride abreast; if any emergency calls for the use of my gun, I can pass Dot to you in an instant; you must remember too, that I have a revolver, which may serve me better in any sudden peril."

"I obey," she replied, "but you will not deny me the right to think you are committing a mistake; since, however, it is actuated by love, I appreciate it."

"I assure you," he said with deep feeling, "that aside from the consideration due you, I am acting for the best. I wish you, as long as possible, to remain at my side. We have made so many turnings and changes in our course that I have lost all idea of the points of the compass; I do not know whether we are going toward Fort Meade or straying off to the right or left, with the probability that in the morning we may be far out of the way. Help me to keep our bearings."

And husband and wife rode out on the prairie in the darkness and falling snow.

CHAPTER XVIII.

NIGHT AND MORNING.

By this time the snow lay to the depth of several inches on the earth. It was still falling, and the cold was increasing. The flakes were slighter, and there were fewer of them. His knowledge of the weather told the rancher that the fall would cease after a while, with a still further lowering of the temperature. Thanks, however, to the thoughtfulness of his wife more than himself, they were so plentifully provided with blankets and extra garments that they were not likely to suffer any inconvenience from that cause.

Fortunately for them and greatly to their relief, the stretch of prairie which they had struck continued comparatively level. Occasionally they ascended a slight elevation or rode down a declivity, but in no case for more than two hours was either so steep that the ponies changed their gait from the easy swinging canter to a walk.

Once, after riding down a slight decline, they struck another stream, but it was little more than a brook, so strait that a dozen steps brought them out on the other side with little more than the wetting of their animals' hoofs.

They rode side by side, for the mare was as fleet and enduring as the horse. Now and then they glanced back, but saw nothing to cause alarm, and hope became stronger than before.

"We are doing remarkably well," said the husband, breaking the silence for the first time in a half hour.

"Yes," was the thoughtful reply; "we must have travelled a good many miles since the last start, and there is only one danger that troubles me."

"What is that?"

"The probability—nay, the almost certainty—that we are not journeying toward the fort."

"I have thought much of that," replied the husband, giving voice to a misgiving that had disturbed him more than he was willing to admit; "it is as you say, that the chances are against our proceeding in a direct line, but it is equally true that the general course is right."

"How can you know that?"

"Because we have crossed two streams that were in our path, and they remain behind us."

"But," reminded the thoughtful wife, "you forget that those same streams are very winding in their course. If they followed a direct line, we could ask no more proof that we are on the right track."

"True, but it cannot be that they take such a course that we are travelling toward the ranch again."

"Hardly as bad as that, but if we are riding at right angles in either direction, we shall be in a sad plight when the morning comes. The sun will take from us all chance of dodging the Sioux so narrowly as we have done more than once since leaving home."

"We must not forget the peril of which you speak; at such times I trust much to the instinct of the animals."

"And would not that, in the present case, lead them to go toward rather than from home?"

"I'm blessed if I thought of that!"

The rancher was filled with dismay for the moment, and brought Dick down to a walk.

"No," he added the next moment, striking him into a gallop again, "if they were left to themselves they would try to make their way to the ranch, but they have been under too much guidance, and have been forced to do too many disagreeable things, for them to attempt that. I am sure we are nearing Fort Meade."

"I trust so," was the response of the wife; which remark did anything but add to the hopefulness of her husband.

The animals now began to show signs of fatigue. The snow balled under their hoofs, causing a peculiar jolting to the riders, when it became so big that the weight broke it or made their feet slip off, when new gatherings commenced immediately to form.

After being forced to a canter the horses would drop of their own accord to a walk, and soon they were left to continue at their own gait.

"How far, Molly, do you think we have come?" asked the rancher.

"It must be fifteen miles, and possibly more; if it were in a direct line, adding what we made before crossing the last stream, it would be safe to wait until morning."

Again the wife gave expression to the thought that was in her husband's mind. He had been asking himself for the last half hour whether it would not be wise to come to a halt for daylight. The rest thus secured to the animals would

95

enable them to do much better, when the right course could be determined with absolute certainty, and a few hours' brisk riding ought to take them beyond all fear of their harassing enemies.

There remained the haunting fear of their being on the wrong course. If daylight found them little nearer the fort than when at the ranch, their situation would be most critical. But all speculation on that important matter must remain such until the truth could be learned.

One reason why the rancher did not propose a halt before it was hinted at by his wife, was that no suitable place presented itself. It would not do to camp in the open plain, where there was no shelter for them or their animals; they must keep on until the ground changed.

That change came sooner than they anticipated. The ponies were plodding forward with their loads, when, before either of the riders suspected it, they were on the edge of another growth of timber, which promised the very thing they sought.

"Here we are!" said Mr. Starr, "and I think we can say that the journey will be suspended until daylight."

"If there is another stream, George, I shall feel safer if we place ourselves on the other side before we halt for the rest of the night."

"I don't view another fording with much pleasure, but we can soon find out how it is."

The character of this timber differed from that which they had already passed, in that it abounded with so many bowlders and rocks that, after penetrating it a short way, it became too dangerous for the ponies to persevere. They were liable at any moment to break a limb.

"Remain here a few minutes while I investigate," said the rancher, passing the sleeping Dot to his wife.

He penetrated more than a hundred yards, without coming upon any water. He did not go farther, for he was satisfied there was none near them. The ground not only grew more rocky and precipitous as he advanced, but steadily rose, so as to show that he was at the base of a ridge over which it was a difficult matter to make their way. It would have been folly to try it in the darkness, and on his return he sought some spot favorable for going into camp.

He was more successful than he expected. A mass of rocks was found, whose tops projected sufficiently to afford a fair shelter. The snow, slanting from the other direction, left a comparatively large surface bare. Here the ponies were drawn to one side and their trappings removed. There were not enough spare blankets to cover them as the fugitives wished to do, but they were too tough to suffer much.

Then the blankets were distributed, and so placed that when the husband and wife huddled together against the base of the rocks, they, as well as Dot, were quite comfortable. The rancher might have gathered wood and started a fire, but it was not needed, and they feared the consequences of such a proceeding. They were so worn out with the trials and toil of the night, that they soon sank into a deep slumber which lasted till morning. Then, upon awaking, the first act of the rancher was to ascertain his bearings, so far as it was possible to do so.

The result was the disheartening conviction that they were no nearer Fort Meade than when they forded the last stream early on the preceding night.

CHAPTER XIX.

A STARTLING SURPRISE.

We must not forget that young Warren Starr and Tim Brophy have an important part to play in the incidents we have set out to relate.

We left them in the wooded rocky section, where they had spent the night together in the rude shelter erected a year before when on their hunting excursions. They were awakened by the frenzied cry of the young Irishman's horse, and appeared on the scene just in time to save the pony from a grizzly bear, who made things exceedingly lively for the young gentlemen themselves.

But relieved of their peril, they sat down like sensible persons to make their morning meal from the lunch brought thither by Tim. They ate heartily, never pausing until the last particle of food was gone. Then they rose like giants refreshed with new wine.

"Now," said Warren, "we will mount the ponies, and instead of making for the fort will try to find the folks."

"I'm wid ye there, as I remarked previously," was the response of the brave young rancher, who was ever ready to risk his life for those whom he loved.

"It will be an almost hopeless hunt, for father could give me only a general idea of the course he meant to take, and we are likely to go miles astray."

"We shall have to depind on Providence to hilp us, though it may be the folks are in no naad of our assistance."

"I pray that such may be the case," was the fervent response of Warren, accompanied by a sigh of misgiving. "I think we shall be able to take care of ourselves, but father is in a bad fix with mother and Dot on his hands. I hope Plummer has joined them."

"He niver will do the same," remarked Tim gravely.

"Why do you say that?"

"He has been killed by the spalpeens, for if he hadn't, he would have showed himsilf before we lift the ranch."

"It looks that way, but you cannot be certain."

"I wish I couldn't, but he must have larned of thim being so near the house as soon as mesilf, or very nearly so, and he would have been back before me.

That he didn't come is proof to my mind that he niver will—ye may depind on the same."

This brief conversation took place while the youths were saddling and mounting their horses. They made certain that everything was secure, and then, carefully guiding their animals among bowlders to the open prairie, paused a moment to decide upon the best course to take.

To the northwest stretched the white plain in gentle undulations, and in the clear sunlight, miles away in the horizon, rose the dark line of a wooded ridge, similar to the others described, and which are so common in that section of the country. They agreed that the best course was to head toward it, for it seemed to them that the rancher had probably crossed the same at some point, or if he had not already done so, would ride in that direction. Possibly, too, the father, despite the wishes he had expressed, would suspect such a movement on the part of his son. If so, the probability of their meeting was increased.

The air was clear, sharp, and bracing, with the sun shining from an unclouded sky. It was a time to stir the blood, and had not the young ranchers been oppressed by anxiety for their friends, they would have bounded across the plain in the highest possible spirits. The ponies, having no such fear, struck into a swinging gallop of their own accord, which continued without interruption until more than half the intervening distance was passed. All this time the youths were carefully scanning the wooded ridge, as it rose more distinctly to view; for they could not forget that they were more likely to meet hostiles than friends in that section, and approaching it across an open plain, must continue conspicuous objects to whatever Sioux were there.

"Tim," said Warren, as they rode easily beside each other, "unless I am much mistaken, a fire is burning on the ridge."

"Where?"

"Almost directly ahead, but a little to the left; tell me whether you can make it out."

The Irishman shaded his eyes with one hand, for the glare of the sun on the snow was almost blinding, and after a moment's scrutiny, said:

"Ye are right; there is a fire up there; not much smoke does the same give out, but it is climbing up the clear sky as straight as a mon's finger."

"I take it that it means Indians; it seems to me they are all around us."

"I agraas wid ye, but s'pose it is a fire that yer fayther has started himsilf."

Warren shook his head.

"He would not do so imprudent a thing as that."

"But he moight have in his eye that we'd be looking for something of the same."

Still his friend was unconvinced.

"He could not be certain that it would be noted by us, while he must have known that it was sure to attract the attention of the Sioux. No; I cannot be mistaken."

"Do ye want to pass it by widout finding out its maaning?"

"If it is father who has kindled the blaze, and he is looking for us, he will find some way of telling us more plainly——"

"Do ye obsarve?" asked Tim, in some excitement.

Beyond question the approach of the two young horsemen had produced an effect. The faint column of smoke which, until that moment, had climbed perpendicularly up the sky, now showed a wavy appearance, vibrating from side to side in graceful undulations, as though it were a ribbon swayed by human hands. But Warren, instead of accepting this as did his companion, regarded it as more indicative of danger. The Sioux that were responsible for the ascending vapor were aware of the approach of the couple, and were signalling the fact to others whose whereabouts was unknown to the whites.

"Do ye moind," said Tim, "that two months since, whin we were hunting along the Big Cheyenne and got separated from him and Plummer, he let us know where they were in jist that way?"

It was a fact. Precisely the same signal had been used by the parent to apprise his son and companion where he and Plummer were, though in that instance it was the employé who adopted the method.

He was inclined for a few seconds to agree with his companion; but there was something in the prominence of the artifice, and the certainty that it would be noted by unfriendly eyes, that caused him to dismiss the belief. Enough doubt, however, had been injected into his mind to bring the desire for further investigation.

"We will ride straight toward it, as though we intended to go to the camp or signal fire as it may be, but will turn aside before reaching the ridge, so as to avoid the trap that may be set for us. I had an experience yesterday afternoon something like that before you joined me."

Strange it was that the couple, who, despite their youth, had learned so much of border life, forgot to keep watch of the rear, while giving so much attention to the front. Singular as it may seem, they had not looked behind them for the preceding half hour. The sight of the signal fire ahead so absorbed their interest that they neglected this obvious precaution; nor did it once occur to them that if the smoke was sent into the sky by hostiles, who meant it for the guidance of confederates, those same confederates were likely to be to the rear of them.

Such was the fact, and the knowledge came to the friends in the most startling manner conceivable, being in the shape of several rifle bullets which whistled about their ears. Then, when they glanced affrightedly around, they saw fully a dozen Sioux bucks, all well mounted, bearing down upon them at full speed.

They had issued from the rocky section behind them, and ridden to this perilous position without the youths once dreaming of the fact until, as may be said, the hostiles were literally upon them.

CHAPTER XX.

A RUN FOR LIFE.

But one thing could be done: that was to run, and Warren Starr and Tim Brophy did it in the highest style of the art. They put their ponies to their utmost pace without an instant's delay. The animals, as if conscious of their peril, bounded across the snowy plain on a dead run, with their riders stretching forward over their necks to escape the bullets expected every moment.

It must have been that the Sioux were sure the fugitives would look around the next moment, else they would have stolen nearer before announcing their presence in such a startling fashion.

The only hope for the young ranchers lay in the speed of their horses, since there was no other possible chance against the bucks who were as fierce after their lives as so many ravening wolves. The boys shouted to their animals, who flew across the plain as though the snow did not discommode them in the least. They did not separate, for the instinctive resolve thrilled them that they would fall or escape together.

Each was provided with a repeating Winchester, and enough has been told to prove they knew how to use the weapons effectively, but the opportunity was hardly the present, since to turn and fire while their ponies were on the run, offered little chance of success, and was liable to interfere with their speed, so important above everything else.

The flight was so sudden that, without thought, they headed toward the wooded ridge, where they had seen the suspicious signal fire, but they had not gone far before discovering that that would never do. The flight must end at the ridge, where they would find themselves at fearful disadvantage.

"We must have the open plain or we are lost!" called Warren.

"Ay, ay; I'm wid ye," replied Tim, who pulled sharply on the right rein of his animal. At the same moment his friend turned the head of his horse to the left, and, before the comrades were aware, they were diverging with several rods between them.

Warren was the first to perceive the mistake, and believing he had adopted the right line of flight, shouted for his friend to do the same. Tim had already noticed the turn and now thundered across the prairie toward him. But the devious course, as will be readily seen, threw him slightly to the rear, seeing which, Warren drew in his animal to allow him to come up.

"None of that!" called the Irishman; "ye've no advantage to throw away! Ye can't hilp me by that nonsense."

But Warren gave him no heed. The next minute Tim was almost at his side.

"I belave we're riding faster than the spalpeens," he added, glancing for the twentieth time to the rear, where the Sioux were forcing their horses to the utmost. They did not fire for some time after the opening volley, giving their whole attention to this run for life.

That the capacities of the pursuing ponies varied was quickly apparent. Several began dropping to the rear, but more than half maintained their places near each other.

It was hard to tell whether they were holding their own or gradually drifting back from the fugitives. The one hopeful fact was that as yet they were not gaining. Whether they would do so or lose ground must quickly appear.

Tim Brophy now performed a deed as reckless as it was daring. He watched the rear more than did Warren, and was in the act of drawing up beside the latter, when he discovered that one of the Sioux was leading all the rest. He was fully a rod in advance, and what was more alarming than everything else, he was gaining, beyond question, on the fugitives. His horse had developed a burst of speed that no one anticipated.

Rising to the sitting posture in the saddle, Tim brought his gun to his shoulder.

"Don't do that!" admonished Warren. "You have no chance to hit him, and will cause Billy to lose ground."

The Irishman made no reply; he was too much occupied with the act he had in mind. Furthermore, he noted that the buck whom he held in such fear was making ready to fire.

But Tim was ahead of him, and, by one of those strange accidents which sometimes happen, he hit him so fair and hard that, with the invariable cry of his race when mortally hurt, he reeled sideways and fell to the ground, his horse, with a snort of alarm, circling off over the prairie far from his companions.

TIM'S FORTUNATE SHOT.

Warren glanced around at the moment the gun was discharged and could hardly believe his own eyes. He knew the success was accidental, and hoped it would not encourage Tim to repeat the attempt.

It was expected that the shot would serve as a check to the rest, and ordinarily it would have done so, but it produced not the slightest effect in that direction. Back of the fallen warrior, whose body rolled over and over in the snow, as it struck with a rebound, were more than half a dozen, with the others streaming after them. They gave no heed to their fallen leader, neither uttering any outcry nor firing in return, but pressing their ponies to the highest possible point. They were resolved upon capturing those fugitives and subjecting them to a punishment beside which shooting would be a mercy.

It would not do to forget the country in front. While their chief interest lay to the rear, they were liable to run into some peril that would undo all the good gained by outrunning their pursuers. Warren saw that while they had swerved to the left, yet the course of the ridge would carry them to its base, unless they diverged still more from the direct path.

And yet this divergence must be made as gradual as circumstances would permit, since otherwise great advantage would be given their enemies by the chance to "cut across lots," or in other words to follow a straight line, while offsetting the curved course of the fugitives.

Directing the attention of Tim to the situation, he begged him to give no further thought to firing upon their foes.

"I'll let the spalpeens alone if they'll do the same wid me," was his reply, spoken in a low voice, for the two were separated by only a few feet.

"You can't have as good luck a second time."

"But," persisted Tim, "if I hadn't dropped that felly, he would have tumbled you or mesilf out of the saddle, as he was about to do whin I jumped on him wid both feet."

But Warren begged him to desist, confident as he was that any further attempt would result in ill to them. Tim held his peace, but leaving his friend to watch where they went he gave his chief attention to the Sioux, whose leaders, if they were not gaining ground, seemed to be holding their own.

Suddenly, to Warren's disgust, his companion again brought his gun to his shoulder. Before he could aim and fire, however, one of the bucks discharged his weapon and the bullet nipped the leg of young Starr, who continued leaning forward, so as to offer as little of his body as possible for a target.

Tim fired, but more than likely the ball went wide of the mark.

His companion hoped that the act of their pursuers in shooting was caused by their fear of losing the fugitives through the speed of their ponies.

But a short distance was necessary before the boys were riding in a line parallel with the ridge that had loomed up in their path. This gave them an open country for an unknown distance, over which to continue their flight, but it was hardly to be supposed that it would continue long. The section was too broken to warrant such a hope.

It may have been the perception of the fugitives' object that brought the shot from the Sioux. At any rate, if it should become manifest that the young ranchers were drawing away, the rifles of the pursuers were certain to be brought into effective use. and the distance between the parties was fearfully brief.

CHAPTER XXI.

AWAY WE GO!

One recourse was before the pursuing Sioux from the start: that was to shoot the horses of the fugitives. The wonder was that they had not aimed to do so from the first. With the couple dismounted, they would be at their mercy.

It was the fear of this that caused Warren to ask his friend to draw up as near to him as he could. It was not likely that both ponies would fall at once, and the survivor might be able to carry the couple to safety.

"I tell ye we are gaining," said the Irishman, with far more hope in his manner than Warren thought was warranted.

"We must gain a good deal before getting out of the woods," was the reply of the other, who devoted every energy to forcing his animal to his best pace.

"Look out! they're going to shoot again," said Tim.

Throwing himself forward, Warren hugged his pony closer than ever, his companion doing the same, instead of trying to use his gun. The volley came while the words were in course of utterance, but neither of the youths was touched. The Sioux must have found it equally hard to fire with their animals on a full run.

"Why don't the spalpeens save their powder?" was the disgusted question of Tim, but his feelings changed a minute later, when his own pony showed by his actions that he had been hit hard. He uttered a low, moaning cry, and staggered as if about to fall.

Warren was the first to notice it.

"Tim, Billy is going to drop; ride closer and mount Jack behind me."

"Not a bit of it! I'll see you hanged first," was the characteristic reply of the brave fellow, who sturdily refused to heed the urgent appeal of his friend.

"Why not?"

"Jack can't carry us both."

"He can until we reach the ridge."

"But we're not going toward it," insisted Tim, too observant to be deceived.

"Turn Billy's head that way," said Warren, growing desperate in the imminence of the peril, and swerving his pony to the right; "Jack can carry us both as well as one."

Still the Irishman hesitated. It might be as his companion said, but he was unwilling to imperil Warren, and destroy the chances of both, when everything looked so favorable for one.

Meanwhile, the stricken Billy was fast giving out. He struggled gamely, but it was evident that he must quickly succumb. At the most, he could go but a short distance farther.

The Sioux fired again, but nothing was accomplished. If Jack was hit, he did not show it during the few seconds that his rider held his breath.

Still Tim held back in the face of the pleadings of his friend. Two discoveries, however, led him to yield.

They were now heading straight for the ridge, which was barely half a mile distant. It must soon be attained, unless something happened to Jack. The foremost Sioux had fallen so perceptibly behind that there was reason to believe the horse could carry both riders to safety, or rather to the refuge which they hoped to find at the base of the ridge.

"I'll do the same, being it's yerself that asks it——"

"Quick! Billy is falling!" called Warren, far more excited than his companion.

The crisis had come. The poor animal could go no farther, and was swaying from side to side like a drunken person, certain to fall with the next minute.

Tim released his foot from the stirrup on his right, swung his leg over the saddle, as only a skilful horseman can do, and, holding his gun with one hand, grasped the outstretched one of Warren and made a slight leap, which landed him behind him.

It was a delicate and difficult task, and despite the skill with which it was executed, both came within a hair of tumbling headlong to the ground.

Quickly as it was done, it was not a moment too soon. The mortally wounded Billy suddenly went forward, his nose ploughing up the snow and earth, and after a few struggles all was over.

The action had not only increased the danger of both of the fugitives, but it rendered the situation of the Irishman doubly perilous. Although both leaned forward, they could not do so as effectually as when each was on his own horse, and Tim of necessity was the more exposed of the two.

Leaving Warren to guide and urge Jack, he gave his attention to the Sioux, who did not relax their efforts, but whose relative situations, owing to the varying speed of their horses, underwent a curious change of position.

Two were riding abreast, and so far as Tim could see there was not the least difference in the speed of their ponies. Behind them at a distance of several rods came two others, holding precisely the same relative positions, while the rest were strung along over the prairie, until it looked as if the hindmost was a third of a mile distant.

Nothing was to be feared from them, but what of those that were so much nearer?

That was the vital question that must soon be answered.

While the position of the Irishman was anything but pleasant, and with the horse on a jump he was required to take the utmost care to maintain his seat, he decided to try his gun once more.

This proved harder than he supposed. He could make no use of the saddle in which young Starr sat, and when he sought to turn he would have fallen, had he not kept one arm about the waist of his friend. And yet, in the face of all this, he managed to get his Winchester in position with the muzzle toward the leading Sioux.

Anything like aiming the weapon was out of the question, and it would have been folly to expect that a second chance shot would favor him. Nevertheless, the demonstration accomplished something unexpected. He had done execution with one shot, and when the bucks saw the muzzle pointing backward, they were scared.

The leaders naturally supposed they were the ones intended to serve as targets, and they ducked their heads with such suddenness that the Irishman grinned. Not only that, but one of them caused his pony—probably through some inadvertent act on the part of the rider—to swerve from his course, thereby interfering with those immediately in the rear.

Even the companion at his side was thrown somewhat out of "plumb," and lost a few paces, much to the delight of Tim, who gleefully told Warren of what had taken place.

The advantage to the fugitives will be understood when it is remembered that they were rapidly drawing near the ridge, now at no great distance in front.

True, there was no certainty that it would prove a refuge to them, if attained; but it would be more of a shelter than the open prairie, where, if driven to bay, there was not the slightest protection against the bullets of the Sioux, unless the body of Jack should be used as a breastwork.

The confusion of the bucks was only temporary. They needed no one to tell them what the aim of the youths was when they changed the line of their flight, nor could they fail to see that the ridge would be attained quite soon, unless they were checked.

Tim Brophy suspected that such thoughts were passing through their minds, and despite the hopelessness of the effort, he discharged his rifle toward them; and when it is stated that it was discharged "toward them," no more can be said. There is no reason to believe that he came within twenty feet of hitting any one of the Sioux.

It may be doubted, therefore, whether this essay on his part was beneficial to himself and companion, inasmuch as it must have lowered their opinion of his marksmanship and convinced the red men that they were altogether mistaken in giving heed to any more shots fired by him from the back of the pony, which was not only going at full speed, but was carrying a double burden.

CHAPTER XXII.

ON FOOT.

The fugitives were now so close to the ridge that Warren Starr, from his position on his pony, turned his attention to their immediate front. He saw that the race must end, so far as his steed was concerned, within the next second. The trees stood close together, the ascent was steep, and the bowlders and rocks, plainly discernible, since all leafage was gone, showed that the horse must halt of necessity at the moment of striking the base of the elevation.

The Sioux had ceased firing. They were so certain of capturing the youths that they saved their ammunition. The struggle could not last much longer.

"Be ready to jump off!" said Warren to his companion; "I am going to stop!"

Even as he spoke, he threw Jack on his haunches with a suddenness that would have pitched the couple over his head, had they not braced themselves. Both took a flying leap from his back and dashed for the cover now directly before them.

The purpose was still to keep together, but circumstances beyond their control prevented. They had no time to form any plan. Young Starr darted to the right, aiming for some rocks which he fancied might afford partial shelter. Tim had his eye on a somewhat similar refuge to the left, and made for that. He would have joined his friend had he known his intention, but the seconds were too precious to allow it, after a few steps were taken. So he kept on without once glancing behind him.

Still there was no firing. The Indians must have felt more certain than ever of their prey, thus to hold their shots. They emitted several whoops of exultation, and the foremost bounded from their ponies and sped after the fugitives like so many bloodhounds.

But the separation of the latter compelled a division of the former, who, it will be remembered, were scattered at varying distances, only a couple being at the heels of the young ranchers. Thus it came about that each was pursued by a single warrior, and through a whim which cannot be fully understood, the Sioux next to the leaders turned to the left on the trail of the young Irishman, who had thus the honor, if it may be so considered, of attracting the greater attention.

For a few moments Warren devoted his energies to running. He bounded like a hare over the first bowlder that interposed, swerved slightly to the right, to pass an obstructing rock, and went up the slope with the same headlong speed with which he had dashed from the level ground to the bottom of the slope.

It was not until he had sped fully a hundred yards in this furious fashion that he ventured to throw a glance over his shoulder. Then he learned that there was but a single Sioux in sight.

The fugitive had held his own so well against this miscreant, that the latter must have felt a quick fear of his escaping him altogether. Young Starr was an unusually swift sprinter, and it may be doubted whether the fleet-footed Indian could have run him down in a fair contest.

The fear of losing the young man caused the Sioux to check himself abruptly, bring his gun to a level, and let fly.

An extraordinary accident, or rather providence, saved the fugitive. At the very instant of his enemy firing, Warren's foot slipped in the snow, and he stumbled on his hands and knees. Certain that his fall was due to the bullet just sent after him, the Sioux, with a whoop of triumph, bounded forward over the bowlders and around the rocks to finish him.

Warren saw, with lightning-like quickness, that his fall might be his salvation. It had deceived his foe into the belief that he was either killed or mortally hurt, and he was, therefore, unprepared for that which followed.

The youth did not attempt to rise. He had slipped down in such a position that he was hidden from the sight of his pursuer. He quickly shifted around so as to face him, and, rising on one knee, held his Winchester pointed and ready for use.

He had not long to wait. The Sioux was so close that the next minute his head and shoulders appeared above the rock, as he took his tremendous strides toward the lad, whom he expected to see stretched helpless on the snowy earth.

The sight of him kneeling on one knee, with his rifle aimed, his eye ranging along the barrel, and his finger on the trigger, was the first startling apprisal of the real state of affairs.

The warrior instantly perceived his fearful mistake, and made a desperate attempt to dodge to one side, but though the loon may elude the bullet of the hunter's rifle, no man has ever yet been equal to the task. No screeching Indian was ever hit more fairly, surprised more suddenly, or extinguished more utterly.

THE DEATH OF THE INDIAN.

And so it came about that in the twinkling of an eye Warren Starr was left without a pursuer. Not a solitary Sioux was in sight.

But he was too wise to think he was safe. He was simply relieved for the time being of his harassing foes. They must have heard the discharge of his rifle, and some of them would soon investigate when their comrade failed to return to them. This would be after a few minutes. Naturally they would suppose that the fugitive had been brought down, and not until a brief period had elapsed would they suspect the truth.

It was this interval which must be utilized to the utmost, if the youth hoped to escape. While the snow would reveal his trail so plainly that it could be followed without the least difficulty, yet his own fleetness ought to enable him to keep so far in advance of the Sioux that they could not gain another shot at him. True, he was deprived of his matchless pony, but the red men were also on foot, and therefore they stood on equal terms, with the opening in favor of the fugitive.

Warren would have been full of hope and resolution, but for Tim Brophy. His concern for his devoted friend forbade him turning the situation solely to his own account. He made a hasty examination of his rifle, and found nothing the matter with it. It was ready for use whenever needed.

Not a solitary warrior was in sight, and the profound stillness which reigned caused the incidents of the last few minutes to seem like some wild dream.

With that peculiar doubt that sometimes comes over one in such crises, Warren gently pinched one hand with the other. The result convinced him that everything was real—imagination had nothing to do with it.

The reports of his own Winchester and the Sioux's rifle were all that had broken the stillness since the headlong leap of the young ranchers from the back of the pony. There could have been no other report without its being heard by Warren, who was sorely perplexed over the fact.

Could it be that equally good fortune had befallen Tim Brophy? Had he been able to throw his pursuers off the track for the time? It seemed impossible that two such providences should come simultaneously to the fugitives. The Irishman was by no means as fleet of foot as Warren, and with the majority of the pursuers dashing after him, only the worst result was to be feared.

"Some of them will soon be here," was the conclusion of the youth, as he stood sorely perplexed as to what he should do; "if I remain, I shall have half a dozen of them around me, and then it will be all up; but what about Tim?"

In his chivalrous devotion to his comrade, he now began withdrawing from his dangerous position, but trended to the right as he faced his enemies, with the object of getting near Tim, and with the hope that he might be of help to him in his desperate strait.

He shuddered as he glanced down at the ground and observed the prints he made in the snow. There could be no delay in tracing him, no matter what direction he might take. It must be the same with his friend, who, despite any advantage gained at the beginning of his last flight, could be readily run down, if the Sioux preferred that to "winging" him while in full flight.

CHAPTER XXIII.

DOWN!

Meanwhile Tim Brophy found himself in the hottest quarters of his life.

Inspired by the same desperate thought of his friend, he strove, with all the energy he possessed, to widen the space between himself and his pursuers. Less fleet of foot than they, it took but a few seconds to show him the hopelessness of the task.

None of the trees was large enough to give protection to his body, but seeing no rocks that could serve him, he dodged behind the first trunk that presented itself. This was barely six inches in diameter, and was no better than nothing at all.

Pausing but a moment, he leaped away again, with that wild, aimless impulse which comes over one when panic-stricken. The halt, brief though it was, proved fatal. His pursuer was on his heels, and the brave youth turned at bay. As if fate was against him, when he attempted to bring his rifle to a level, he made a slip and it dropped from his grasp. He had no time to pick it up.

"S'render! s'render!" called his foe in good English, waving his right hand aloft with his gun grasped in it.

"I'll surrender, ye spalpeen!"

Resorting like a flash to nature's weapons, the Irishman delivered a blow straight from the shoulder, which sent the Sioux spinning backward with his feet pointing toward the sky.

Had he been the only foe to contend with, Tim might have saved himself, for the savage was utterly "knocked out," and the opportunity to finish him could not have been better.

Tim had his revolver, but in his excitement he forgot the important fact. He was about to leap upon his prostrate enemy, with the intention of snatching his gun from him and using it, when the other two Sioux burst to view.

Without waiting for them to assail him, the youth dashed forward like a panther at bay.

Before the foremost could elude the assault, he struck him as fairly as he had hit the other, and he sprawled on his back, with the breath driven from his body.

But the impetus of his blow carried Tim forward, and, half tripping in his headlong rush, he fell on his hands and knees. He strove frantically to save himself, but, before he could struggle to his feet, the other Sioux dealt him a stroke with the butt of his gun which laid the fellow helpless on his face.

The skull of the Irishman, however, was tough, and he quickly recovered, but not before several other warriors appeared on the scene.

For one moment the young rancher meditated a rush upon them, and had actually doubled his fists for that purpose, but even in his fury he perceived the folly of such a course. If he assailed the Sioux, they would quickly finish him then and there, while the fact of their having spared his life thus far proved that they did not intend to put him to instant death.

It was with singular emotions that he recognized among the last arrivals the Carlisle student Starcus, who had saved his life the preceding morning by his timely shot when the grizzly bear was upon him. The presence of the "civilized" youth among the hostiles told its own story.

"Ye've got me foul," said Tim, looking straight at Starcus as he spoke; "and now ye may do wid me what ye loikes."

Starcus, knowing the words and look were meant for him, made no answer, but kept in the background.

He was grim and silent. Who shall say what thoughts were stirring his heart at that trying moment! He had sat with this youth at the table of George Starr and his family.

He had partaken of their hospitality, and had claimed to possess the civilization which he was anxious his own race should adopt, but here he was, taking part in the pursuit and attack of two youths who not only had never done him harm, but had always acted the part of friends toward him.

There was one curious fact (and yet, perhaps it was not so curious after all) which was evident to the captured youth. The Sioux admired the brave fight he had made for himself. Trained for ages to regard physical prowess as above all virtues, the American race cannot fail to revere it, even when they are the sufferers therefrom.

The warrior who had first felt the weight of Tim's fist now began clambering to his feet. He was dazed and bewildered, for the blow was a terrific one. Landing squarely in his face, it had brought considerable crimson, which, mingling with the daubs of paint already there, gave him a frightful appearance.

He assumed the upright posture, and standing uncertainly for a few seconds, fixed his eyes on the prisoner.

Then grasping the situation, and recognizing him as the individual that had treated him so harshly, he suddenly emitted a shout, whipped out his hunting-knife, and rushed at him like a fury. Tim instantly threw himself into a pugilistic attitude, and no doubt would have given a good account of himself had he been permitted, for he was skilled in the art of self-defence, and such a person always has the advantage over a foe, no matter what his weapon, provided it is not a firearm.

But the collision did not take place. Three Indians interposed, restraining the fierce red man; among the foremost being Starcus, who roughly seized the upraised arm and forced the warrior back several steps, using some strong words in his own language. The savage strove to free himself that he might attack the youth, but he was not permitted, and finally gave up the effort and withdrew sullenly into the background.

This incident was hardly over, when the second warrior that had gone down before the young Irishman's prowess also gained his feet. He looked as if he would very much like to try conclusions again, with the aid of one of his weapons, but he seemed to think he could bide his time, and have it out on a more fitting occasion.

The captive was too wise to place a favorable construction on the interference of Starcus, despite the additional fact of his kindly offices of the morning. The rest of the Sioux had shown a wish to take him prisoner, for certainly the chance to bring him down had been theirs more than once. Actuated by their intense hatred of the white race, they looked upon sudden death as too merciful to a foe that had done them so much ill. He had slain one of their best men, and knocked prostrate two others; no punishment, therefore, was too cruel to be visited upon him.

While the group stood about the helpless captive they talked in their own language, without Tim being able to guess the meaning of a word uttered. He watched the countenances closely, and was surprised a minute or two later by the appearance of the last member of the party. He came straggling up as though he felt no concern in the proceedings. That which interested Tim the most was the sight of his valued Winchester in the fellow's hand. For one moment the youth thought he meant to hand it over to him, but that would have been a stretch of hospitality of which none of his race could ever be guilty. He did a rare thing for an Indian—indulged in a grin of pleasure at the prize which his companions had passed by to allow it to fall into his possession.

In his trying situation, Tim Brophy could not avoid a feeling of curiosity concerning Starcus. To him the fellow's conduct was inexplicable. While his presence among the Sioux was proof that he was "with them" in thought, intention, and feeling, yet there was the friendly act of the morning during the struggle with the grizzly, and his late interference to prevent the warrior from injuring him, which united to puzzle the captive.

As has been said, he was too wise to build much hope on these facts, but nevertheless they raised doubts and questions relating wholly to the future.

Would Starcus continue to hold his present enmity to the people that had been friendly to him?

While he had been carried away by the frenzy that had driven so many of his people out of their senses, was not an awakening likely to take place, when his better nature would resume control? Could he forget that he had eaten salt with this hapless fellow, and stand by, without raising hand or voice, when his extremity should come, as come it must, in a very brief while?

But these were questions that Tim Brophy could not answer; they must be left for the immediate future.

CHAPTER XXIV.

THE FRIEND IN NEED.

While these lively scenes were taking place, Warren Starr was not idle. The report of his gun was plainly heard by the other Sioux and the captive, but the former took it for granted that it was fired by their comrade, and calmly awaited his return with the news of the death of the fugitive.

But as the reader has learned the boot was on the other leg. The youth was unharmed, and his enemy was of no further account.

Actuated by the chivalrous wish to help Tim, he began cautiously picking his way along the slope, at a considerable distance from the base, peering forward and listening intently for sights and sounds that could tell him how his companion had fared.

He had better fortune than he dared expect. The flickering of something among the trees warned him that he was in a delicate position, and his farther advance was with the utmost care, accompanied by glances on every hand, to guard against walking into a trap.

Very soon he reached a point from which he saw all that was going on. Tim was standing defiantly among the Sioux, who appeared to be discussing the question of what to do with him. He identified Starcus, and recognized also the hapless state of affairs.

Much as he regretted the conclusion, Warren Starr was forced, in spite of himself, to see that it was out of his power to raise a finger to help his friend. For one moment he meditated bringing his Winchester to his shoulder and opening fire, but at the best he could not hope to bring down more than two or three before the others would be upon him. With no possible way of escape open, the situation of Tim would be worse than before, for one of the first things done by the Sioux would be to slay him on the spot, whereas they were now likely to spare him for a time, and so long as he had life, so long did hope remain.

Warren would have been as eager to befriend the brave fellow as the latter would have been to aid him; but, as we have said, there was no dodging the fact that it was out of his power. What, therefore, should he do for himself and the other loved ones for whom all this danger had been incurred?

Where were that father, mother, and little sister? They might be in equally sore distress, and longer delay on his part perhaps would decide the question of life or death.

Stealthily withdrawing again, until well beyond sight of the group, he began carefully descending the side of the ridge toward the open prairie. In doing so, he avoided doubling on his own trail, for at any moment some of the Sioux were liable to start out on a tour of investigation, which would bring them face to face with him.

With all his senses on the alert, he threaded his way among the trees and around the rocks and bowlders, until he stood on the base of the elevation, with the broad plain, across which he and his friend had fled in such desperate haste, stretching out before him for many miles.

But another sight interested him. Along the foot of the ridge were scattered nearly a dozen Indian ponies, cropping as best they could the grass, whose tops faintly showed above the thin coating of snow. Their owners had abandoned them in their haste, without thought of securing them to any of the limbs, confident that they would be found within reach when wanted.

They were tough little animals, without saddle or bridle. The majority had a blanket roughly secured over the back, with a thong about the upper part of the neck, which was all that was needed to guide them wherever their masters willed.

But there was one animal worth all the rest for whom the eyes of the youth eagerly searched among the group, scattered at varying distances. He would have given anything for a sight of his own Jack at that moment.

To his astonishment, he saw nothing of him. Through some unaccountable cause, he had vanished as utterly as if he had never existed.

In the vain hope of discovering him, Warren glanced from one to the other, until he had surveyed each one several times over. But there was no mistake; Jack was invisible.

The fact caused him keen regret, but it would not do to tarry, with the certainty that the Sioux would soon learn the truth and be after him like a whirlwind. One or two of their ponies were almost as fleet as Jack, and Warren was a good enough horseman to ride them as well as their masters could without saddle.

Fixing his attention on the best looking animal, which happened also to be the nearest, he moved briskly toward him, with the purpose of bounding upon his back and dashing away; but his abruptness defeated his intention. It frightened the pony, who with a snort threw up his head, trotted several rods out on the prairie, and then turned and looked at him.

The alarm of this animal communicated itself to the others, who also hurriedly trotted beyond his reach.

The situation was critical. The action of the ponies was almost certain to be heard by their owners a short distance off, and they would be quickly on the spot. If they caught sight of the youth on foot trying to steal one, his position would be far more hopeless than when among the rocks and trees.

Seeing his mistake, Warren tried to right matters by a less abrupt approach. He dropped to a slow walk, holding out his hand and uttering soothing words. Had he done this at the beginning, he would have had no trouble in capturing any horse he desired, but the animals identified him as a stranger, and continued shy.

The finest, which he had sought first to catch, closely watched him as he slowly approached, but at the very moment the heart of the youth was beating high with hope, he swung his head around and trotted beyond reach. Warren turned his attention to the one that was nearest, and by a sudden dash aimed to catch his halter, one end of which was dangling in the snow.

As he stooped to grasp the thong, it was whisked from under his hand, and the pony galloped beyond his reach.

The bitter disappointment made Warren desperate. He had undertaken an impossible task. He might succeed had more time been at his command, but the Sioux were liable to appear any minute. It would not do for him to be caught in this situation. He must abandon the attempt and get back among the trees and rocks, where there remained the bare possibility of eluding the red men.

"What the mischief has become of Jack?" he muttered, facing about and breaking into a lope for the ridge. "If he were only in sight, he would come to me at once. Hello! just what I feared!"

At that juncture he detected something moving among the trees. It was not clearly seen, but not doubting that the Sioux were coming, he broke into a run for cover, not daring to risk a shot until partial shelter was secured.

In his affright he did not dare glance to the left even, and held his breath in thrilling expectancy, certain that with every leap he took he would be greeted by a volley, or that the Sioux would throw themselves across his track to shut off all chance of escape.

That they did not do so was not only unaccountable to him, but gave him the hope that possibly he might still elude them. Bending his head, he ran with might and main. The distance was not great, but it seemed tenfold greater than it was, and a slip of the foot, which came near bringing him to his knees, filled his heart with despair and made him certain that he would soon join Tim Brophy.

He heard his pursuers at his heels. Despite his own fleetness, they were outspeeding him. Nothing could save him from being overtaken before reaching the ridge.

Suddenly a peculiarity in the sound made by those at his rear caused him abruptly to halt and look around.

Then, to his unbounded delight and amazement, he recognized his own pony, Jack, striving hard to keep him company.

CHAPTER XXV.

THE PRAIRIE DUEL.

Warren Starr could have hugged his pony in his transport of delight. Until a moment before he was sure several of the Sioux were upon him; when, wheeling about, he was confronted by Jack, whom he had been desirous of meeting above every other person or animal in the world.

The action of the horse he understood. On the sudden flight of his master he had attempted to follow him among the rocks and trees of the ridge; the Indians, in the flurry of the occasion, paying no attention to him. Failing, he was making his way back to the open prairie, when the sight of his master sent him galloping after him; Warren being too panic-stricken to suspect the truth until he was well-nigh run down by the faithful animal.

"Heaven bless you, Jack!" he exclaimed, with glowing face and joyous heart; "you are in the nick of time."

Saddle and trappings were unharmed, though the tapering limbs of the creature had been scratched and cut by his attempt to follow his master. The youth was in the saddle in a twinkling, and, but for the sad situation of Tim Brophy, he would have uttered a shout of triumph.

For in truth he felt safe, even though the hostiles were dangerously near. Remembering this, he rode farther out from the ridge, and whooped and swung his arms at the Indian ponies, who dashed still farther out on the plain.

It was inevitable that this tumult should become known to the captors of Tim Brophy. Young Starr expected it, and therefore was not surprised when he saw the figures of several warriors at the base of the ridge. He could not forbear swinging his Winchester over his head and taunting them. They replied with several shots, but the distance was too great for Warren to feel any alarm. He, too, discharged his gun at the group, and acted as if he meant to challenge them to come out and attack him.

If such were his intentions, the challenge was accepted. Several warriors ran out on the prairie, calling to their ponies, in order that they might mount and take up the pursuit. Their action caused the youth no alarm, for the test of speed had already been made, and he feared none of the Indian animals.

The latter may have been under good discipline when their masters were astride of them, but they showed anything but obedience now that they were free from their control. They kept trotting about in circles, and avoided the warriors with a persistency that must have been exasperating to them.

Only one displayed consideration for his master. He was among the fleetest, and after some coy dallying he stood still until the athletic Sioux came beside him. He vaulted upon his back, and then accepted the seeming challenge of the youth.

The latter had checked his steed at a safe distance on the snowy plain, and confronted the Indian party. Looking beyond the warrior nearest him, he strove to catch sight of Tim Brophy; but he was too far off, and the trees interfered with his vision. Before he could continue the scrutiny long, the mounted Sioux demanded his attention.

Prudence would have suggested that now, since young Starr was well mounted, he should take no chances, but scurry away at the top of his speed, leaving the discomfited warrior to nurse his chagrin over the clever trick played upon him.

But the young rancher saw no reason why he should flee from a single buck, no better mounted or armed than himself. He had had enough experience in the Northwest to understand those people well, and thought he knew how to take care of himself. No, he would fight him; and now opened a most extraordinary prairie duel between Warren Starr and his dusky enemy.

The youth glanced at his Winchester, and saw that it was all right, as was the case with his revolver. His saddle was firmly cinched in place, Jack was at his best, and what cared he for a single Indian, even though he was a warrior that had taken the scalp of more than one unoffending pioneer!

Jack stood as motionless as a statue, with his nose toward his enemy. A gentle wind blowing across the prairie lifted his luxuriant mane slightly from his neck and swung his heavy tail to one side. His head was high, and the nostrils seemed to breathe defiance to the dusky foe, who approached at a swinging gallop, as though he meant to ride down the animal and rider.

But he held no such intention. The Sioux required no one to tell him that that stationary figure, sitting so firmly in his saddle, meant to fight.

While more than a hundred yards still separated the combatants the Sioux horseman wheeled to the right, and, without checking his speed, started to describe a long circle around the youth. The latter spoke softly to Jack, who slowly turned, so as to keep his head continually pointed toward the enemy. Evidently the animal understood the situation, and was competent to do his part.

The Sioux at the base of the ridge had given over their effort for the time to capture their ponies. All their attention was centred on the two horsemen out on the prairie.

As yet the Indian made no move to fire. Warren was looking for him to throw himself over the side of his animal, and aim from under his neck, screening his own body meanwhile from the bullet of the young rancher. Instead of doing so, however, he described a complete circle about Warren, coming back to his starting point, while Jack continued to move around, as if on a pivot, keeping his head always facing his foe.

The warrior was starting on his second round, when, without any perceptible movement, he discharged his gun. Warren saw the blue puff of smoke, the report sounding dull and far away in the wintry air.

The bullet did not pass nigh enough for him to be aware how close it was. It would seem that the Indian ought to have done better, for it was noticeable from where Warren sat that in completing his circle he had shortened it, and was now several rods nearer than when he set out to circumnavigate him.

"It is no more than fair to return the compliment," thought Warren, raising his Winchester, taking careful aim, and pulling the trigger. Truth compels us to say, however, that his shot went as wide of the mark as the one aimed at him. Thus far honors were equal between them.

The Sioux continued his trip around the central object, though what he expected or hoped to accomplish by this curious proceeding was more than his antagonist could conjecture.

The advantage during the performance possibly was with young Starr; for, by keeping the nose of Jack pointed toward the other he offered the least possible target to the foe, while the course of the Indian compelled him to hold his pony broadside, himself remaining a conspicuous object on his back.

"I think I can shorten this business," reflected Starr, "by another shot or two. I am standing still, and if I can't bring that fellow off his horse I'm of little account."

But the Sioux was more watchful than he suspected. Hardly was the Winchester raised when, presto! the warrior disappeared. He had flung himself far on the other side of his pony, and was capable of maintaining that situation while making the circuit of the youth.

The latter held his fire. He was confident of being able to hit the other animal, but to his mind that would be taking a dishonorable advantage, though none knew better than he that he was dealing with an enemy to whom treachery was a cardinal virtue.

The horse showed no decrease of his speed, but continued galloping forward with the easy swing shown by the trained circus animal when an equestrian is giving an exhibition. That the rider, from his position on the other side of his body, with his moccason extended over the spine of the animal, was keeping close watch of the youth the latter did not need to be told.

He must have seen Warren, after holding his weapon levelled for a moment, lower it again, disappointed at the vanishing target. The next moment the Sioux discharged his weapon.

CHAPTER XXVI.

ON THE GROUND.

The aim of the warrior was better than before, and though it was not fatal, it came startlingly near being so. The bullet nipped the ear of the pony, and cut through the coat of Warren Starr; grazing his shoulder in the passage.

There could be no question that the red man was in dead earnest, and that when he discharged his rifle he meant to kill.

It must not be supposed there was any holding back on the part of the youth; he was equally resolved that, if the chance were given, he would do his best to bring his antagonist from the back of his horse.

The Sioux resumed his circling course, gradually drawing nearer the young man, who continued as alert as at the first; ready to take advantage of any opening that presented itself.

Suddenly the red man wheeled his pony in the opposite direction, doubling on his own course. This compelled him to swing over to the other side in order to continue his use of the animal as a shield. He executed the movement with wonderful deftness, but a singular condition was against him.

Young Starr had just formed the decision that the best, if indeed not the only thing he could do, was to shoot the steed of his foe. This was easy, and with the Indian dismounted he would be at a great disadvantage, though likely still to use the body of his animal as a guard against the marksmanship of his enemy; but the latter counted on the flurry giving him his opportunity.

Thus it happened that at the moment the Winchester was at Warren's shoulder, and his eye was ranging along the barrel, he caught a glimpse of the dusky body in the act of whisking over that of the pony. The glimpse was only momentary, but under the peculiar conditions it was just what was needed. The youth fired, and with such accuracy that the warrior lunged over his steed, and sprawled in the snow on the other side.

The released animal threw up his head with a snort, and trotted toward the ridge as if he, too, had felt the sting of the bullet and was hastening away from a possible repetition.

The sight of the Indian on the ground told the youth of the success of his shot, but it did not lead him to do anything rash, as would have been natural in the flush of triumph. The Sioux was not yet killed, and was still capable of mischief.

Warren rode rapidly a few yards toward him, and then brought Jack to an abrupt halt. He had seen something suspicious in the actions of his enemy.

"Is he shamming?" was the question he asked himself, as he leaned forward, carefully keeping the head and neck of Jack in front of his body, and on the alert against a treacherous shot.

The Sioux seemed to have fallen on his side, with his face turned partly away from the youth. With surprising quickness he shifted his position so as to confront the horseman, and still lay prostrate in the snow, as if unable to rise.

There might be a sinister meaning to this. The pretence of being mortally disabled was an old one with his people, as many a white man has learned when too late. If he were trying the artifice in the present instance, he did it skilfully.

Under the belief that he was powerless to inflict further harm, nothing was more natural than that the youth should ride forward with the purpose of giving him his quietus, disregarding his own safety until a bullet through the body should apprise him of his fatal oversight. It was this fear that checked Warren in the very nick of time.

The one great obstacle in the way of the Sioux successfully playing this ruse was that he was in open view, where no movement on his part could be concealed. Were it in the wood, with rocks and trees at his command, the chances would have been far better for him.

Warren Starr kept his eye fixed on him. It would have been easy, while seated on his own pony, to drive a ball through the miscreant, who was fully exposed to his fire, but it might be after all that he was badly wounded and unable to defend himself. If such were the case he could not commit the cruelty of firing at him again, even though the Sioux would have eagerly seized such a chance against a foe.

It was for the purpose of learning the truth in the matter that Warren watched him with the utmost closeness, holding his own weapon ready to use the instant the other made a hostile demonstration.

The action or rather inaction of the other Sioux at the base of the ridge was suggestive, and increased the suspicion of the young rancher. They were in a direct line with the one on the ground, so that Warren readily saw them without withdrawing his attention from his immediate antagonist.

Instead of rushing out to the help of the latter they remained where they were, and continued the role of spectators. This looked as if they did not believe the fellow was in need of assistance, and they were simply waiting with confidence in the result of the piece of treacherous cunning.

The warrior with his left hand drew his rifle round to the front. The weapon was a magazine one like Warren's, and it was one, therefore, of which it would not do to lose sight.

The gun being in position for use, the owner, apparently with difficulty, raised the upper part of his body, so that it was supported on the left elbow. Then he essayed to call the right hand into play, but appeared to find a difficulty in doing so.

Up to this moment Warren Starr had been trying to learn in what manner the fellow was wounded. The motion of his lower limbs showed no weakness, though it might have been there without appearing, so long as he held his prone position and did not call them into use.

The action now indicated that his right arm was the one that had suffered, since it fumbled awkwardly and refused to give the needed help when called upon.

Still all this might be pretence, intended to deceive the youth into uncovering himself. Warren did not lose sight of that probability.

The action of the Sioux was precisely what it would have been had he, knowing that he was confronted by a merciless enemy, done his utmost, while badly wounded in the right arm, to bring his weapon to bear upon him. There was no hesitation or trouble with the left arm, but it was the other which, from appearances, refused to answer the call upon it.

It was seen to move aimlessly about, but still was unable to help in aiming, and the hand could not manipulate the trigger—an impotence which, if actual, was fatal.

But who can trust an Indian? Knowing that his slightest action could not escape the keen eyes of the youthful horseman a short distance away, was he not likely to direct every movement with the purpose of deceiving him?

The truth must show itself soon; but be it what it might, Warren Starr had the comforting belief that he was master of the situation. He was unharmed, with his ready Winchester in such position that he could use it like a flash. As yet the Sioux had not brought himself to the point of aiming, and Warren was watching him so closely that he could anticipate his firing. He was resolved that the instant he attempted to shoot he would let fly, and end the singular prairie duel.

It has taken considerable time to make all this clear, but the incidents from the fall of the Sioux to the close occupied but a few minutes.

Young Starr spoke in a low voice to his pony, who began moving slowly toward the prostrate Indian, the rider holding his weapon ready as before. Jack took short and very deliberate steps, for he did not like the appearance of things. A man lying on the ground is always a disquieting object to a horse, and this one had already felt the sting of the Indian's anger when the bullet clipped a tiny speck out of his ear. Warren Starr was resolved to learn the truth, and he did so before Jack had advanced a dozen steps.

CHAPTER XXVII.

A GOOD SAMARITAN.

The young rancher was yet some distance from the prostrate foe, when his quick eye discovered something. It was a crimson stain on the snow near the stock of the Indian's rifle.

The miscreant was wounded; he was not shamming.

It was remarkable that with this discovery came an utter revulsion of feeling on the part of the youth. While he had been ready up to that moment to drive his bullet through the bronzed skull, an emotion of pity now took possession of him. He forgot that the fellow had tried with desperate endeavor to take his life, and he knew he expected no mercy at his hands. Nevertheless, as a Christian, he could not withhold his sympathy, nor could he forget that simple but sublime role of the good Samaritan.

Touching his heels against the ribs of Jack, the pony increased his pace, but had not yet reached the prostrate figure when Warren experienced the greatest surprise of all.

The Indian on the ground was Starcus!

The next moment young Starr dropped from his saddle, and was bending over him.

"I hardly expected this, Starcus," he said, with a gentle reproof in his voice. "You seem to have changed your mind since this morning, when you shot the grizzly."

Indian though he was the fellow's painted face was darkened by an expression of deep pain, whether the result of his hurt or of his mental disquietude no one can say.

"I am not your friend; I am the enemy of all white men."

"You have proven that since you turned against those who would do you no harm. But I have no wish to reproach you; your arm is badly hurt; let me give you what help I can."

"I want no help," replied the Sioux, resolutely compressing his thin lips; "go away and leave me alone."

"I shall not; I am your master, and shall do as I please with you."

"I tell you to leave me alone; I do not want your help," added Starcus fiercely.

"You shan't hinder me, old fellow; this is for old times."

And paying no heed to the sufferer, who struggled with pitiful awkwardness to keep him off, Starr ripped a piece from the lining of his coat, and began bandaging the bleeding arm. The Sioux still resisted, but while doing so showed a weakness rare in one of his race by fainting dead away.

The youth made no effort to revive him until he had completed his hasty but rude swathing of the arm, which was badly shattered by a bullet. Then he flung some snow in the face of the fellow, who had already shown signs of coming to.

Starcus looked around for a moment in a bewildered way, and then fixed his gaze on the wounded member, now bound so that the flow of blood was stopped. Then he turned his dark eyes on the face of the youth bending over him, with an indescribable expression, and said in a low voice:

"I tried my best to kill you, Warren."

"But you didn't; and I am unharmed, and am your friend."

"And why are you my friend? I do not deserve it," continued the Sioux, with his black eyes still centred on the face of the athletic youth.

"If you and I had what we deserved where would we be? Give it no further thought."

Starcus now held his peace for a full minute, during which he never once removed his gaze from the countenance of the good Samaritan. Strange thoughts must have passed through his brain. When he spoke it was in a voice as gentle as a girl's.

"Can you forgive me for what I have done?"

"With my whole heart."

"But I tried my best to kill you."

"Are you sorry?"

"Yes, sorry as I can be."

"Then I repeat, I forgive you; but are you able to rise to your feet?"

"Yes; I pretended I was not, so as to bring you closer to me. Had not my arm been hurt I would have shot you."

"I am not sure of that," replied Warren, with a curious smile; "I suspected it, and was on my guard. At the first move on your part I would have fired. I was not sure even that you were hurt at all until I saw blood on the snow. But it will not do for you to stay here. Let me help you to your feet."

Starcus proved that the rest of his limbs were uninjured by coming as nimbly as an acrobat to an upright posture.

"You have done all you can for me, and I thank you; now do not wait any longer."

"Why not?" asked Warren, suspecting his meaning, but desirous of testing him a little further.

"Look toward the ridge," was the significant reply.

The inaction of the other Sioux, as has been intimated, was due to their belief that Starcus was master of the situation. Even when they saw him pitch from the back of his pony they must have thought it a part of the strategy designed to lure the young man to his death.

But the sight of the youth bending over the prostrate figure of their comrade told the truth. Starcus had been wounded, and was at the mercy of his conqueror.

Much as the warriors were disappointed, they were not the ones to allow the brave fellow to be killed without an effort on their part to save him.

Warren had suspected the truth, and, while seeming to be unaware of it, he observed several of the warriors running at full speed from the ridge out on the snowy prairie. They were still a goodly distance away, and he calculated just how far it was prudent to allow them to approach before appealing to Jack, standing within a few paces and awaiting his pleasure.

He was hoping for just such a warning from Starcus as he had received. He wanted it as a "guarantee of good faith," and when it came all doubts of the sincerity of his repentance were gone.

Still, although this particular Sioux might feel gratitude for the undeserved mercy shown to him, there was no hope of anything of that nature from his companions. Had Warren counted upon that, he would have made the mistake of his life. He and his friend had done the bucks too much ill to be forgiven for an act of kindness to one of their number, even though it was actuated by a motive whose nobility they could not fail to understand.

"That is kind of you, to warn me of my danger," remarked the youth. "I shall not forget it. But they are so far off that I need not hurry to mount my horse."

"Do not wait too long; they will soon be here."

"I have my pony, and they are on foot."

"But they can run fast."

"I will leave in time; but, Starcus, if you are really a friend of mine, you have the chance to prove it by being a friend of Tim; he is a prisoner with your people, and in need of your good offices."

"I cannot help him," was the reply, accompanied by a shake of the head.

"I only ask that you shall do what you can; I am sure you will, whether it results in good to him or not."

"Give yourself no hope of that; it will be hard for me to explain why I was spared by you."

"But that was my own affair; surely they cannot suspect us of any collusion."

"You do not know my people as I do."

"But I am not the first white man that has shown mercy to a helpless foe; they know that as well as you and I."

"You are waiting too long, Warren; they will soon be here," added the warrior, with an apprehensive glance toward the ridge, from which his people were approaching with alarming swiftness.

"Well, good-by, Starcus."

He grasped the left hand of the Sioux, who warmly returned the pressure with the words, "Good-by, Warren."

Then Warren Starr, not a moment too soon, sprang into the saddle and galloped away.

CHAPTER XXVIII.

THE LONE HORSEMAN.

The young rancher had calculated matters closely, for hardly was he in the saddle when the foremost of the running Sioux halted, raised his gun, and fired. He was nigh enough to make his shot dangerous, though providentially it did no ill.

It was an inviting chance for Warren to return the fire with the best prospect of doing so effectively. But he had no disposition to slay any one of the hostiles. His singular experience with Starcus had a softening effect, and he was resolved to attempt no injury against the men unless compelled to do it in actual self-defence.

Jack, being put to his best paces, quickly carried him beyond any further peril, and when far enough to feel safe he checked the pony and looked back.

He saw half a dozen Sioux gathered around the wounded Starcus, evidently in conversation. Being strong in his lower limbs, and with his wounded arm bandaged as well as it could be, he required no attention or help from them. After all, knowing the buck had been a close friend of the young rancher, they must have seen nothing remarkable in the mercy that had been shown to him. White men are as capable of meanness and cruelty as the Indians, but few of them disregard the laws of honorable warfare, and still fewer are deaf to the cry of a hapless foe.

A few minutes later the group moved slowly back in the direction of the ridge. A couple, however, drew off, and began a more systematic hunt of the ponies that had shown such a fondness for their freedom. They managed matters with such skill that they soon coaxed a couple of the fleetest back to captivity. With the aid of these they soon corralled the others, and the party gathered with their animals at the base of the ridge.

Warren Starr remained at a safe distance for the greater part of an hour, in the hope of learning something of the intentions of the Sioux. But they gave no sign that he could understand. The ponies were in plain sight near the trees, and he caught glimpses of their owners moving back and forth, but nothing could be learned as to what it all meant.

He now debated what he should next do. He was free, well mounted, and at liberty to follow his own judgment.

His immediate anxiety was concerning Tim Brophy. He knew he was in the most perilous strait of his life; Warren's parents might be as badly situated, but he had no knowledge of the fact. He therefore hoped for the best concerning them. But if there was any way of helping his friend it was beyond his power to discover it. He was a prisoner in the hands of a dozen watchful and treacherous Sioux, who were not likely to give him the least chance of escape, and any attempt on the part of Warren to befriend him would not only be utterly useless, but would imperil his own life.

He had appealed to Starcus to make the effort, but Warren saw the force of the Indian's declaration that it was beyond his power. He was wounded himself, and at the first move to interfere in behalf of the captive, who had killed one of their best warriors and badly bruised a couple, would be likely to bring down their vengeance upon his own head. Distressing as was the conclusion, there was no escaping it—he must turn his back on his devoted comrade. Warren accepted the situation like a martyr, and had decided to continue his search for his folks, of whose whereabouts he had only the vaguest idea.

Two lines of action presented themselves, and there was much to be said in favor of and against both. By sharp riding he could reach Fort Meade before sunset, and there whatever help he might need would be cheerfully given by the commandant. Under the guidance of the friendly Indian scouts, they could search for the rancher and his family; and their knowledge of the people, as well as the country, would render such search far more effective than any by the youth, without taking into account the force that would insure safety instantly on such discovery.

But this plan involved considerable time, with the certainty that his folks must spend another night in imminent peril—a night that he could not help believing was to prove the decisive one.

Knowing nothing of the death of Jared Plummer, Warren hoped that he was with his father, despite the gloomy prophecy of Tim Brophy. If the young rancher could join them, the party would be considerable, and ought to hold its own against any band of Indians such as were roaming through the country. Besides, all would be well mounted and prepared for flight whenever advisable.

These and other considerations, which it is not necessary to name, decided the youth to make further search for his folks before riding to Fort Meade.

One fact caused him no little speculation. It will be remembered that the approach of himself and Tim to the ridge was caused by the discovery of a thin column of smoke climbing into the sky from a more elevated portion than that attained by themselves or the Sioux with whom they had had the stirring encounter.

He did not forget, either, that the red men with whom they had exchanged shots, and from whom he had escaped by the narrowest chance conceivable, appeared from the opposite direction. Neither then, nor at any time since, had anything occurred to explain the meaning of the vapor that had arrested their attention when miles away.

If it had been kindled by Sioux or brother hostiles, why had they not appeared and taken a hand in the lively proceedings? Abundant time was given, and if they were there they ought to have met the fugitives at the close of their desperate chase, when they sprang from the back of Jack and dashed among the trees on foot.

It was these questions which caused the youth to suspect that the fire might have been started by his father. True, he had expressed a disbelief in this view when given by Tim, but that was before the later phase had dawned upon him.

It looked like a rash act on the part of the rancher, if he had performed it, but there might be excuse for his appealing to the signal that he had employed in a former instance to apprise his son of his location.

Speculation and guessing, however, could go on forever without result. There was but one way of learning the truth, and that was to investigate for himself.

Prudence demanded that the Sioux at the base of the ridge should be given no inkling of his intention; and, in order to prevent it, a long detour was necessary to take him out of their field of vision.

Accordingly he turned so as to follow a course parallel to the ridge, and breaking into a swift canter kept it up until, when he turned in the saddle and looked back, not the first sign of the hostiles was visible.

He was now miles distant, too far to return on foot, even had he felt inclined to abandon Jack and try it alone. He rode close to the base of the ridge, whose curving course was favorable, and facing about started back toward the point he had left after his survey of the party that held Tim Brophy a prisoner.

He did not believe there was any special danger in this, for he had only to maintain a sharp lookout to detect the Sioux, if they happened to be journeying in that direction. The broad stretch of open plain gave him every chance he could ask to turn the fleetness of Jack to the best account: and he feared no pursuit that could be made, where he was granted anything like a chance.

His purpose was to approach as near the spot as was prudent, provided they remained where he last saw them, and then, dismounting, penetrate nigh enough to learn the meaning of the smoke which was such an interesting fact to him. The task was a difficult one, for it was more than probable that by the time he reached the neighborhood of the signal fire it would be extinguished; for certainly his father would not continue the display after it had failed in its purpose, and the appearance of the hostiles showed him that it was liable to do more harm than good.

CHAPTER XXIX.

A BREAK FOR FREEDOM.

Accustomed as are the Sioux to scenes of violence, it is not probable that any members of the party to whom we have been referring ever looked upon a sight so remarkable as the prairie duel between Starcus and the young rancher.

This Indian, who had come among his native people in the hope of staying the tide of frenzy sweeping through the tribe, was himself carried away by the craze, and from a peaceable, well-educated youth became among the most violent of those that arrayed themselves against the white man.

It was one of the better impulses of his nature that led him to fire the shot when Tim Brophy was in such danger from the grizzly bear; but, as he afterward confessed, it was no sooner done than he reproached himself for not having turned his weapon against the two youths for whom he had once entertained a strong friendship.

When the headlong Irishman started toward him, Starcus hurried away, and not only joined a band of prowling hostiles, but told them of the lads, and joined in a scheme to capture and hold them as hostages for several turbulent Sioux then in the hands of the Government authorities. Knowing them as well as he did, he formed the plan of stealing up behind them, while they were riding across the snowy prairie, and the partial success of the plan has been shown.

His comrades watched the opening and progress of the strange duel with no misgiving as to the results. They saw how a run of wonderful fortune had helped the young rancher, but now, when something like equality existed between the combatants, the superiority of the American over the Caucasian race must manifest itself.

As events progressed the interest of the spectators deepened. They descended to the edge of the plain, where the view was unobstructed, leaving but a solitary warrior guarding the prisoner. The solicitude of the latter for his friend was as intense as it could be, for he could not be sure of the result until the end. He feared that Warren Starr was committing the same rashness for which he had often chided him.

The view from the rocks through the intervening trees was so imperfect that it grew to be exasperating, but there seemed to be no help for it.

The warrior in charge of Tim Brophy was expected to give his full attention to him, but as events progressed there was danger of his forgetting this duty. He began to look more to the singular contest than to his captive.

This Indian was standing on his feet, leaning forward, and peering as best he could between the trees and the obstructing limbs. Tim was seated on a bowlder at his side, and until this moment was the target of a pair of eyes that would have detected the slightest movement on his part.

The Irishman was quick to observe that by the strange trend of events a golden opportunity had or was about to come to him. The warrior seemed to forget him entirely, though, like all his people, he would be recalled with lightning quickness on hearing or seeing anything amiss.

Surely no such chance could come again. Convinced of this, Tim seized it with the rush of a hurricane.

Rising quickly and noiselessly to his feet he delivered a blow as quick as a flash under the ear of the Sioux, which stretched him like a dead man on his face.

There had been no noise, and in the excitement of the occasion the Indians at the base of the ridge were not likely to learn what had taken place until the revival of the senseless warrior, who was not likely to become of any account for several minutes.

Tim needed no urging to improve his opportunity. Facing the top of the ridge, he started off with a single desire of getting over the rough ground as fast as possible.

He had taken but a few steps, however, when he abruptly stopped.

"Begorra!" he muttered, "but what a forgitful spalpeen is Tim Brophy!"

He had no rifle. That would never do, when pursuit was inevitable in a short time. Accordingly, he turned about, ran to the prostrate figure, and took the gun from his grasp. It was not as good as his own, but inasmuch as that was in the possession of one of the others it was beyond recovery.

It seemed cruel, but to make matters safe the Irishman gave the prostrate fellow a second vigorous blow, from which he was certain not to recover for a considerable while.

"I hate to hit a man whin he is down," he reflected. "If I meets him ag'in I'll ax his pardon."

It was no time to indulge in sentiment, and he was off once more.

Some strange fate directed his steps, without his noticing the fact, along the trail made by Warren Starr in his first hurried flight. Thus it was that he came upon the other warrior that had been outwitted by the youth whom he was so confident of capturing.

Urgent as was his hurry, the fugitive paused a moment to contemplate the sight. Then with a sigh he hurried forward, for not a moment was to be lost.

It was remarkable that, after having captured the young man with so much difficulty, they should have invited him to escape, as they virtually did by their action, but the circumstances themselves were exceptional. The like could not happen again.

It was the same curious turn of events that extended his opportunity. It is rare, indeed, that, after a captive does make a break for freedom, he is allowed such a period in which to secure it; but here again the unparalleled series of incidents favored him.

There had been no outcry on the part of the third victim to Tim Brophy's good right arm. But for the forgetfulness of the youth in starting off without his gun, the fellow would have recovered speedily and made an outcry that must have brought several of his confederates to the spot.

But events were interesting beyond compare out on the prairie. All the Sioux but the one named were watching them, and when they saw the plight of Starcus there was a general rush to his assistance. The return was slow, being retarded by the efforts of several to capture their wandering ponies. When they succeeded in doing this and coming back to the edge of the plains, the better part of half an hour had passed.

The first startling recollection that came to the party after this return was the fact that the warrior who had pursued the young rancher up the side of the ridge had not put in an appearance. They would have awakened to this fact long before but for the affair between Warren Starr and Starcus. Now that it was impressed upon them, and they recalled the report of the gun that reached them long ago, together with the reappearance of the young rancher on the back of his pony, they could not fail to see the suspicious aspect of things.

There was a hasty consultation at the base of the ridge, and then the man who was really the leader ordered a couple of his warriors to lose no time in learning the truth. As eager as he to investigate, they set out without delay, but had not gone far when one of them uttered a cry which brought the whole party to the spot.

A striking scene greeted them. The white prisoner was gone, and the Indian left in charge lay on his face like one dead. His gun was missing. Strange proceedings had taken place during the absence of the party.

It took but a few minutes to learn the truth. It was easy to see that the interest of the guard in the incidents on the plain had caused him to forget his duty for the time. The Irishman had suddenly assailed him with that terrible right arm of his, and felled him senseless to the ground.

The recipient of this attention was not dead, but he felt as though he wished he was, when he was helped to a sitting position, and was compelled not only to suffer the pain of the terrific blows received, but had to face the jeering looks of his companions, who could forgive anything sooner than the outwitting of a full-grown warrior by a trick which ought not to have deceived a child.

CHAPTER XXX.

COMRADES AGAIN.

Actuated by his resolution to learn the real meaning of the signal fire seen on the crest of the ridge, Warren Starr pushed on in the face of the fact that every rod in the way of advance increased his own peril. Studying the contour of the country, and carefully making his calculations, he was able to tell when he drew near the scene of his stirring encounter with the war party of Sioux. Deeming it unsafe to ride farther, he drew his pony aside, and, dismounting, led him among the rocks and trees, until he was beyond sight of anyone passing over the open country. He did not forget that a plain trail was left, which would serve as an unerring guide to those hostiles who might come upon it, but that was one of the risks of the undertaking which could not be avoided.

"Now, Jack, my boy, I want you to stay right here till I come back again," he said, in parting from the animal. "You have been faithful and have served me well, and I can depend upon you, for you are sure to do the best you can."

There could be no doubt on that point, and without any more delay he left the creature and began toiling up the ascent, his Winchester firmly in his grasp, and as alert as ever for the sudden appearance of his enemies.

An astounding surprise was at hand.

He had penetrated but a short distance from his starting point when he became aware that someone else was in the vicinity. He caught only a flitting glimpse of a person, who, descrying him at the same instant, whisked behind a bowlder for protection. Warren was equally prompt, and the two dodged out of each other's sight in a twinkling.

"If there is only one Indian," reflected the young rancher, "I ought to be able to take care of myself—great Heavens!"

The exclamation was caused by the sight of Tim Brophy, who stepped from behind the shelter and walked toward him.

Young Starr was astounded, and believed for a minute that his friend had been put forward as a decoy, and that his captors were immediately behind him. But that dread was removed the next moment by the appearance of the young Irishman, who, advancing jauntily, called out in his cheery voice:

"It's all roight, me boy! None of the spalpeens are here, and it's mesilf that would like to shake ye by the hand."

That the two warmly grasped hands and greeted each other need not be stated. Even then Warren could only murmur:

"Why, Tim, this is the greatest surprise of my life! Where in the name of the seven wonders did you come from? and how came you to give them the slip?"

"It was that which helped me out," replied the other, holding up his clenched fist; "it b'ats all other wippons whin ye git into a tight corner."

Not until the fellow had told his story could the other comprehend the amazing truth. Then he saw how a marvellous combination of circumstances had helped him, and how cleverly the quick-witted youth had turned them to account.

"I must shake hands with you again," responded the delighted Warren. "I never knew of anything more remarkable."

"Ye didn't think ye could give me any hilp," chuckled Tim, "but ye did it all the same."

"How?"

"Haven't I told ye that the little circus ye opened out on the plain drew away all the spalpeens but the single one lift to look after me? And don't ye understand that ye made things so interesting that he forgot me until I reminded him I was there by giving him a welt under the ear that he won't forgit in a dog's age?"

"I see; but I never dreamed of any such result as that."

"Nor did I, but it came all the same, and sarved me as will as if ye had fixed up the whole business."

Noticing the strange weapon in his hand Warren referred to it, and then received the whole story.

"Well, it beats anything I ever heard of. Jack isn't far off, and we can use him as we did before."

"And may I ask what ye are doing here so close to the spalpeens, whin ye ought to be miles away?"

"I set out to learn whether that fire whose smoke we saw was started by father or not. I didn't think so when you and I were talking it over, but can't rid myself of the suspicion till I find out for myself."

Tim nodded his head, and said:

"Yis; it was Mr. Starr that did it."

"How can you know that?"

"I've been there, and found out," was the surprising reply.

"Where are he and mother now?"

"Can't say; I'm looking for them. Whin I give the spalpeens the slip I did the best travelling I knew how, and without thinking of anything but getting away as quick as I could I coom right onto the spot where the fire had been burning. It hadn't gone out yit, but it was so nearly so that it give no smoke. Looking around it did not take me long to l'arn that two horses had been there——"

"They had three with them, as you told me."

"But they have only two now. I wouldn't have been sartin of the matter if I hadn't seen the print of yer mother's small shoe in the snow, and while I was looking I obsarved that of Dot, no bigger than Cinderella hersilf might have made."

Warren was profoundly interested, and tears dimmed his eyes.

"Was there no man with father?"

"I couldn't see any footprints except his."

"Then it has been as you said: Plummer was killed by the Sioux. But surely you noticed the direction they took?"

"I did that same, and was following their trail whin I cotched sight of yersilf among the trees, and coom nigh shooting ye before asking for an inthrodoocticn."

"Then they have passed nigh this spot?" asked the startled son.

Tim partly turned and pointed behind him.

"Right beyant is the thracks made by thimsilves and their animals, for the ground won't admit of their riding."

"I wish it were otherwise," remarked Warren thoughtfully, "for I have had the hope that they might be so near the fort as to be safe. They are not, but we ought to join them quite soon. But, Tim," added his friend, as if alarmed by a new fear, "the Sioux must have learned of your flight long ago, and are now on your trail."

"I must say that I'm forced to agree wid ye," was the reply of the Irishman, spoken as though the question was of trifling import.

"It won't do for us to stay here. They are liable to appear at any moment," and the alarmed youth glanced apprehensively around, as if he expected to see the whole party of hostiles burst through upon them.

"Jack is strong enough to carry us a long way," he added, "and since he is close at hand I can lead him out on the open plain, where we shall gain such a good start that there will be little chance of their overtaking us."

"No doubt ye are corrict."

"Then let's do it without throwing away another moment."

He turned hurriedly to carry out his own purpose, when his comrade laid his hand on his arm and detained him.

"I think, Warry," he said, in a low voice, "that ye've forgot one matter—yer fayther, mither, and Dot."

"Gracious! how came I to do that? Here I set out to hunt for them, and when they were as good as found I turn my back upon them, and think only of my own safety."

"Ye are excoosable, since ye have been upsit by the thrifling occurrences that have been going on this day."

"Take me to the spot where you left their trail," added Warren, with unusual excitement, "and we'll never leave it until we join them; we shall escape or die together."

The youths moved like those who knew that the question of life and death must be settled within a few minutes.

CHAPTER XXXI.

THE LAST HOPE.

The young ranchers had to go but a short distance, when they struck the trail left by their friends. The snow rendered it so distinct that the first glance told the story. Warren saw the track made by the feet of his father, mother, and little Dot. The consciousness that he was so near them profoundly affected the son.

"There are several strange things about this," he remarked to Tim, halting for a minute before taking up the search in earnest; "we found it almost impossible for a horse to clamber up the ridge, and yet their two ponies have been to the very crest."

"That's because they found an easy way to do it from the ither side," was the sensible comment of Tim Brophy.

"Of course, but father is away off the track. More than half a day has passed since he left home, and he is hardly a quarter of the way to Fort Meade."

"He is just as near as we are, and he didn't start any sooner," was the significant remark of Tim Brophy.

"But that was his destination when he set out, while our business has been to find him."

"With no moon or stars to guide him last night, what means had he of keeping to the right coorse?"

The question gave its own answer. The cause of this wandering was so self-evident that Warren Starr would not have asked it had he not been in such a state of mental agitation as a person feels when certain he is on the eve of some critical event.

Reasoning with something like his usual coolness, the young rancher thought he saw the explanation of other matters which had puzzled him, but he bestowed little thought upon them, for his whole ambition for the time was to reach his parents.

The trail which they were following led toward the open prairie, left by Warren but a short time before. It was evident that Mr. Starr was making for that, for their animals could not serve them so long as they continued in this rough section.

"If I had been a little later," reflected the son, "I would have met them. That I did not proves that they cannot be far off."

He was tempted to call or whistle, but that would have been rash, for if there was any one point on which he was certain, it was that the hostiles were hot on the trail of Tim Brophy. The real peril was from that direction, and several times he reminded the Irishman of the fact, though he needed not the warnings.

A short distance farther and both stopped with an exclamation of dismay. The report of a weapon sounded from a point only a little way ahead.

"That was not a rifle," said Warren, turning his white face on his companion; "it was a pistol."

"Ye are corrict."

"And it was fired by father."

"I'm sure ye are right."

"They have been attacked! come on! They need our help!"

The youth dashed ahead, clambering over bowlders, darting around rocks, ducking his head to avoid the limbs, stumbling, but instantly regaining his feet, only intent on getting forward with the utmost possible speed.

His companion found it hard work to keep up with him, but fortunately they had not far to run. Without the least warning of what was coming Warren Starr burst upon his astonished parents and little Dot, the rush being so impetuous that the rancher had his Winchester half raised to fire before he understood.

At the feet of Mr. Starr lay the mare dead, killed by her master. While struggling over the rugged places she had slipped and broken her leg. The rancher mercifully put her out of her misery by placing the muzzle of his revolver to her forehead and sending a bullet through her brain.

Mrs. Starr and Dot had turned away that they might not witness the painful sight, for they loved the creature. The arrival of the youths caused the mother to face quickly about, and the next moment she and her son were clasped in each other's arms, with Dot tugging at the coat of her big brother.

"Warren, Warren, I guess you forgot me," she pleaded, when she thought the embrace had lasted long enough.

"Forget you, my darling!" he repeated, catching her up and hugging the breath from her body; "never! we are together again, and only death shall separate us."

The rancher had shaken the hand of Tim Brophy during this little by-play, and they exchanged a few words before father and son closed palms.

Then the questions and answers came fast. Tim Brophy drew a little aside to where mother and child stood, and holding the tiny hand of Dot explained matters, while Warren did the same with his father.

"Did you see us approaching when you started the fire?" asked Warren, after hurriedly telling his own story.

"No, but I was quite sure, when your mother and I came to talk it over, that you would disregard my wishes about hurrying to the fort. We went astray in the darkness, and after a number of narrow escapes, as I have just related, found ourselves at the base of this ridge on the other side."

"Did you recognize where you were?"

"No; the points of the compass were all askew, and to save my life I couldn't get my bearings. But I was convinced that you were at no great distance, and decided to try the signal which Plummer and I had used before. Poor Plummer!"

"Do you know anything about him?"

Mr. Starr related what he had discovered, adding that the body was shockingly mutilated and stripped of its belongings.

"The ascent of the ridge on the other side was quite easy, and we found no difficulty in leading the horses to the crest. There the fire was kindled. Knowing of the long stretch of level ground on this side, we set out without waiting to learn the result of the signal smoke. I knew that if you made your way to the spot where it was burning you would understand the situation, and the snow would show you how to follow us as fast as you desired."

"Did you hear or see nothing of the Indians?"

"We saw nothing of them, and were confident that the party with whom we had repeated encounters were thrown so far behind that we had good reason to believe they need be feared no longer. But all our hopes were scattered when we heard firing from the direction of the open plain. While fleeing from one party of hostiles we had almost run into another. I confess," added the father, "that for a minute I was in despair. Your mother, however, retained her courage, as she has from the first. She urged me to make for the level country, aiming for a point so far removed from the sounds of the guns that we would not be seen, unless some ill fortune overtook us. My haste in striving to do so caused the mare to fall and break her leg. I could not bear the sight of her suffering, and though I knew the danger of the act, I put her out of her misery with a pistol-ball through her brain."

"You little dreamed that Tim and I had a part in the firing of those guns which so alarmed you."

"No; it did not occur to me; but we must not make the mistake of supposing we are yet out of danger."

The experiences that had been hastily exchanged awakened the ranchers to the fact that they were still in imminent peril, for the Sioux were certain to follow Tim Brophy vigorously, and at that moment could not be far off.

Mr. Starr beckoned to his wife and Tim to approach.

"You understand matters," he said, "and the question is, what is best to do?"

"Why not continue our flight?" asked the wife.

"I would not hesitate a second were we not so fearfully handicapped. There are four of us, not counting Dot, and we have but two animals, provided Warren's pony can be found, which I very much doubt. True, we men can walk or take turns in riding, but if we continue our flight, speed is indispensable, and we would make a sorry show in our crippled condition. We would be absolutely helpless on the open prairie against the Sioux, all of whom, Warren tells me, have excellent horses."

The rancher had a scheme in his mind, but before making it known he wished the views of the others.

"It's mesilf that thinks this," said Tim Brophy; "let us go wid yees to the ridge of the prairie, and there mount Mr. Starr on Jack, while Mrs. Starr and Dot can take the ither. Thin, what is to hinder yees from going like a house afire for the foort?"

"But what of you and Warren?" was the natural question of the rancher.

"We'll cover yer retr'at."

"The proposal does more credit to your heart than your head, but I cannot entertain it."

"Nor will I listen to anything which compels us to separate again," added the son decisively. "I do not believe you can reach Fort Meade without another fight, and the absence of Tim and me would destroy hope from the first."

"But my idea," persisted the Irishman, "was to keep the fight away from the folks and have all the fun oursilves."

"That would do if it were possible to arrange the business that way," said Warren, "but the Sioux are the ones who have the decision in their hands, and while we were doing our best others would slip off and attack father and mother. If we remain together it must be otherwise. If there ever was a situation where union is strength this is one of them."

"I've exhausted me resoorces," said Tim, withdrawing a step, as though he had nothing more to say. Leaving the others to decide, he took Warren's Winchester from his unresisting hand, and began watching for the approach of the Sioux, who he was certain were following the trail through the snow.

One fact was apparent to him, and he considered it no unimportant advantage. The pursuers would advance at a speed that must bring them into sight before they could surprise the fugitives.

A glance around showed that the rancher could not have selected a better place for defence. The bowlders were on all sides, there being a natural amphitheatre several rods in extent. Kneeling behind these the whites had a secure protection against their enemies, unless they should make an overwhelming rush—a course of action which is never popular with the American Indian, inasmuch as it involves much personal risk to the assailants.

It was at his suggestion that the others seated themselves on the ground while holding their conference. When the Sioux should appear it would be on the trail made by the party, so that the Irishman knew where to look for them. He, too, crouched down, with the muzzle of the Winchester pointed between two of the bowlders, ready to fire on the first glimpse of a target.

Even the pony was forced to lie down near the lifeless body of his comrade. So it was that anyone might have passed near the irregular circle of bowlders without a suspicion of who were within it.

"I have but the one proposition to make," said Warren, seeing that his father was waiting for him to speak, "and that is to stay here and fight it out. We are strong enough to hold the Sioux at bay for a good while, perhaps long enough to discourage them."

"And what have you to say, Molly?"

"I cannot feel as hopeful as Warren, but it really seems to me that that is the only recourse left to us."

"I do not agree with either of you," remarked the rancher, feeling that the time had come to announce his decision. "I formed my plan some minutes ago. It is the only one that offers the slightest hope, and I shall insist on its fulfilment to the letter. It is that Warren shall leave at once, find his pony if he can, mount him, and ride with all haste to the fort for assistance. Tim will stay behind with us to help fight. The time for discussion is past; we must act. Warren, make ready to leave this minute."

CHAPTER XXXII.

AWAY! AWAY!

When George Starr announced his decision to any member of his family no one presumed to question it. Had the son been disposed to do so in this instance he would have refrained, for he believed, with his parent, that he had made known their last and only hope.

"I will go, father!"

He was in the act of rising to his feet, when Tim Brophy discharged his rifle.

"I plugged him," was his comment, as he peered through between the bowlders; "the spalpeen wasn't ixpicting the same, but that one won't bother us any more."

Being in the act of rising at this moment, Warren shrank back again, undecided for the moment what to do, but hesitation was fatal, as his father saw.

"Go," he said; "don't lose an instant; they are not on that side; you can slip off without being seen."

The youth saw the force of the words. Crouching as low as possible, with the Sioux rifle in his hand, he passed between the bowlders opposite to the point at which Tim had fired, and which, therefore, was in the direction of the open prairie.

The move was one of those in which success depends wholly upon promptness. The Sioux would speedily dispose themselves so as to prevent anyone leaving, as soon as they found that the parties whom they were seeking were at bay among the bowlders. Fortunate, therefore, was it that no delay took place in the flight of young Starr, even though, when he started, the enemy was at the gate.

It required no very skilful woodcraft for him to get away, since it was not anticipated by the Sioux, and he had the best means for concealing himself.

There had been one idea in the mind of the rancher, which he would have carried out but for the sudden appearance of the Indians; that was for his son to take the remaining pony with him. The fugitives could make no use of him, and should it prove that Jack was gone, his owner would not be without the means of pushing to Fort Meade for help. Circumstances, however, prevented that precaution. It never would have done to attempt to take the remaining pony. Warren quickly vanished among the trees and bowlders, and the Rubicon was crossed.

But Jack was found just where he had been left, patiently awaiting the return of his master. The pursuit of Tim Brophy by the Sioux had led them in a different direction, though, had the flight of Warren been postponed for a short time, the steed must have fallen into the hands of the enemy.

The heart of the youth gave a bound of delight when he came upon the animal.

"Follow me, Jack," he said cheerily; "if you ever did your best, now is the time. The lives of us all depend upon you. Have a care, my boy, or you will slip."

In his eagerness the youth descended the slope faster than was prudent. Jack did slip, but quickly recovered himself, and no harm seemed to have been done.

It was but a short way to the edge of the prairie, where the pause was long enough to see that the trappings were right, when the young rancher swung himself into the saddle, twitched the rein, and said:

"Come!"

The gallant fellow, with a sniff of delight, sprang away, and sped with a swiftness which few of his kind could surpass. The snowy plain stretched in front, and he darted over it as though his hoofs scorned the earth. The still air became a gale, which whistled about the ears of the youth, who felt the thrill that comes to one when coursing on the back of a noble horse to whom the rapid flight is as pleasant as to the rider.

It was now near meridian. A long distance remained to be passed, and since a goodly portion of it was rough and precipitous, the young rancher felt little hope of reaching Fort Meade before nightfall.

"If we could have such travelling as this," he reflected, "we would be there in a few hours, but there are places where you will have to walk, and others where it will be hard work to travel at all."

It was a discomforting thought, but it was the fact; since the youth was not following the regular trail leading from the ranch to the fort at the foot of the Black Hills. But his familiarity with the country and the daylight ensured him against going astray; he was certain to do the best possible thing under the circumstances.

Two miles had been passed at this brilliant pace, and Warren was as hopeful as ever, when he became aware of an alarming truth, and one which caused a feeling of consternation—Jack was falling lame. That slip made in descending the lower part of the ridge, just before his owner mounted him, was more serious than he had suspected. It had injured the ankle of the horse so that, despite the gallantry with which he struggled, it not only troubled him, but with every leap he made over the plain it grew worse.

It was a condition of things enough to cause consternation on the part of the rider, for it put an end to his hope of reaching the fort that day. True, he could continue the advance on foot, but, doing his utmost, he could not arrive before late at night—so late, indeed, that no help would be sent out before the morning, and they could not reach the beleaguered fugitives until late on the following day.

"Can they hold out until then?"

That was the question which was ever in the young rancher's mind and which he dare not answer as he believed the probabilities required.

There was no getting away from the fearful truth. The vigilance of his father and Tim might enable them to stand off the Sioux as long as daylight lasted. Each had an excellent magazine rifle, for it will be remembered that he had exchanged weapons with his young friend, but there was not only a formidable party of bucks surrounding them, shutting off all possibility of their slipping off during the darkness, but other Sioux were in the neighborhood who could be readily summoned to the spot.

Darkness is the favorite time with the red men when moving against an enemy, and they would probably make no determined demonstration until the night was well advanced. Then, when they should rush over the bowlders, nothing could save the fugitives. Should this emergency arise, Warren Starr felt that everything was lost, and he was right.

He weakly hoped that Jack would recover from his lameness, but all know how vain is such an expectation. The injury rapidly grew worse, so that when the animal dropped his gait to a trot and then to a walk, Warren had not the heart to urge him farther.

Slipping from the saddle he examined the hurt. It was near the fetlock of the left hind leg. The skin was abraded; the ankle evidently had been wrenched. It was swollen, and when the youth passed his hand gently over it, the start and shrinking of the creature showed that it was excessively painful to him.

"It's no use, Jack," said the lad; "I know you would give your life for me, but you can't travel on three legs, and I'm not going to make you suffer when it can do us no good."

Manifestly there was but one course open—that was to abandon the pony and press on as fast as he could on foot. Jack could get along for a day or two, and his master would not forget to look after him on the first opportunity.

There was no call to burden himself with the saddle and bridle, but they would prove an incumbrance to the animal if left upon him, and his owner was too considerate to commit the oversight.

In riding so fast the young rancher had followed the general course of the ridge, so that on halting he was quite near it. He now turned to his right, calling upon Jack to follow.

The action of the pony was pitiful. When he bore a part of his weight on the limb, after the brief halt, it had become so painful as to be almost useless. Nevertheless he hobbled forward until the foot of the slope was reached.

Here Warren removed the trappings. His blanket being rolled behind the saddle, he spread it over the back of the horse and secured it in place.

"It is all I can do for you, Jack," he said tenderly, "and it will give you protection against the cold. You will be able to find a few blades of grass here and there where the snow has not covered them, and the buds of the trees will give some help. The snow will prevent your suffering much from want of water. Perhaps a good long rest will improve your ankle so that you can use it. If it does," and here the young rancher spoke impressively, as though he expected his steed to understand his words, "I want you to start for the fort; don't forget that!"

He touched his lips to the forehead of his faithful ally, who looked after his young master, as he walked away, with an expression almost human in its affection. But there was no help for it, and with a sad heart, but the determination to do his utmost, Warren Starr resumed his journey toward Fort Meade.

Not long after parting with his pony he came upon something which caused him surprise. In the snow directly in front appeared the footprints of a single horse that had passed over the ground on a run, taking the same direction that the youth was following.

His experience with horses told the youth at a first glance that the animal was travelling at his utmost speed. The trail swerved inward from the open plain, as though the rider had sought the base of the ridge for his protection.

Had there been several ponies coursing ahead of him, he would not have found it so hard to understand matters, for he would have concluded that they were an independent party, making all haste to reach some point, but he could not read the meaning of a single warrior speeding in this fashion.

"Whoever he was he lost no time," mused Warren, breaking into a loping trot, for his own haste was great.

Had he not known that poor Jared Plummer was no longer among the living, he would have thought it possible that he was making for Fort Meade. He wondered whether it could not be a white man engaged on a similar errand.

The probabilities were against this supposition. He knew of no rancher in the neighborhood of his old home, and it would seem that no white man would ride with such desperation unless pursued by a relentless enemy, and he saw no evidence of such a contest of speed.

True, the pursuers might have been farther out on the prairie, but their trail would have joined that of the fugitive ere long, so as to make the line more direct; but though the young rancher trotted a full half mile before checking himself and looking around, he discovered no signs of others.

The last advance of Warren brought him close to the precipitous section which, knowing well, he had feared would prove too difficult for his pony. Raising his eyes to survey it and fix upon the best line to follow, he caught sight of the horseman he had been following.

His animal was on a deliberate walk, and coming directly toward him. The youth stopped short. As he did so he perceived that he was an Indian warrior. Warren brought his rifle round in front, with no intention of running from him or taking advantage of the cover near at hand.

The Indian raised his hand, and oscillated it as a signal of comity. As he did so the two were so near that the youth perceived that the arm was bandaged. Something familiar in the appearance of the horseman struck him at the same moment, and the young rancher lowered his weapon with the exclamation:

"Starcus!"

It was he, and as he rode forward he had a strange story to tell Warren Starr.

CHAPTER XXXIII.

BREAD CAST UPON THE WATERS.

When the Sioux who had rushed out on the open plain to the help of the wounded Starcus gathered around him they were quick to perceive that his life was due to the mercy of his conqueror, but their hostility toward the latter was not diminished one whit by the discovery; they were as eager for his life as ever, and proved it by firing several shots after him as he rode away.

The wounded arm was bandaged in a piece of the lining of Warren Starr's coat. The crimson stain showed through the cloth, though the flow of blood was checked. Sound and unhurt as was Starcus in all other respects, he was unable to use the injured limb, and was therefore as useless in any impending hostilities as if out of existence.

As the party moved back toward the base of the ridge there was a consultation among them as to what was best to do. Starcus expressed a more venomous rancor than ever against the white people, and especially against the one that had brought him low. He regretted that he was to be helpless for weeks to come, with a permanent injury for life.

When the leader of the band suggested that he should return to the nearest village and remain until able to take the warpath again, he vehemently opposed it. He was not willing to retire in such a humiliating manner, but the leader insisted, and after sulking a while the "civilized" Indian consented.

Being a capital horseman, he leaped unassisted upon his pony, and unwilling in his anger so much as to bid the warriors good-by, he struck the animal into a swift gallop, heading toward the village, where he was expected to stay until fully recovered.

The action of the warrior was singular. After riding some distance he glanced behind him at the ridge he had left. He seemed to be in an irritable mood, for he uttered an impatient exclamation and urged his beast to a faster gait. His wound pained him, but the agitation of his mind and his own stoical nature caused him to pay no heed to it. Indeed nothing more could be done for the hurt.

When he looked back the second time he had reached a point for which he had been making since his departure. He was out of sight of any of his people who might be watching him.

An abrupt change in the course of his pony was instantly made, and he sent him flying at the height of his speed. Strange as it may seem, he was aiming for the same point toward which Warren Starr started some time later.

He did not spare his animal. He went like a whirlwind, and as though his life depended upon reaching his destination without delay. Warren Starr read the trail aright when he interpreted it as meaning that the pony before him was going as fast as he could.

Starcus was picking his way, still mounted, over the rough section where the youth had expected to meet great difficulty with his animal, when he suddenly discovered that white people were immediately in his front. He drew up, and was in doubt for a minute whether to flee or hold his ground.

A squad of cavalry from Fort Meade confronted him. They numbered nearly twenty, under the command of a young lieutenant, a recent graduate of West Point. They were accompanied by a couple of Indian scouts familiar with the country.

Starcus was quick to make a signal of friendship, and then rode forward to meet the soldiers, who had halted upon seeing him.

The Sioux was well known to the two Indians, the officer, and several of the cavalry. They knew he had joined the hostiles, and were therefore suspicious of him. This fact rendered his self-imposed task one of considerable difficulty. But after a while he convinced them of his honesty.

The lieutenant had been sent out by the commandant at Fort Meade to bring in the rancher and his family, their scouts having reported them in imminent danger. Starcus explained that the parties for whom they were looking were at no great distance, having left the ranch the night before to hasten to the fort. One of the ranchmen had been killed, and the rest were in great peril. Starcus said he had started to ride to the fort for help, and it was most fortunate that he encountered it so near, when the passing moments were beyond importance.

The young officer was sagacious. He could have asked some very embarrassing questions relating to the wound of the messenger, but he wisely forbore. It is not best at all times to let a person know how much is plain to you and how much you suspect. Evidently Starcus was earnest in his desire to befriend the imperilled ones; the fact that he was journeying alone in the direction of the fort constituting the strongest evidence.

He explained that the ridge where he believed the whites were doing their best to escape the Sioux was much more approachable from the other side. He described the ground minutely, and the two scouts present confirmed the accuracy of his statements.

When the lieutenant proposed that Starcus should act as their guide the truth could no longer be kept back. He made a clean breast of everything.

He had been with the hostiles. He was among the fiercest. He had tried to shoot young Starr, who, more fortunate than he, brought him wounded from his horse. When he lay on the ground, at his mercy, the young man rode up, spoke words of kindness, and bandaged his wound.

And in doing this the youth proved more of a conqueror than he had done by his excellent marksmanship. He won the heart of the Indian, who was now eager to prove his gratitude by any act in his power. He unhesitatingly answered that he would serve as the guide to the cavalry.

But once again the officer displayed rare tact. If Starcus was sincere in his newly awakened friendship for the whites, it might be in his power to accomplish a great deal of good by going among his people and using persuasion and argument; but if he should appear as an active ally of the whites such power would be gone, and it would be unsafe at any time in the future to trust himself among them.

"No," replied the lieutenant; "return to your own people; do what you can to show them the mistake they are making in taking the warpath; you may effect much good. My guides will do as well as you to direct us to the spot where the whites are in urgent need of our help. You say it is not far, and I am hopeful that we shall be in time to save them."

Accordingly Starcus parted from the cavalry, and was on his return to join his people and to attempt to carry out the wise suggestion of the officer, when he encountered the young rancher making all haste on foot to secure the help which was much nearer than he had dared to hope.

After exchanging friendly greetings, Starcus told the story which the reader has just learned.

Warren listened with amazement and delight. He had, indeed, heaped coals of fire upon his enemy's head by his forbearance, and the bread cast upon the waters had returned before many days.

"You have acted nobly," was the comment of the youth.

"Can it undo the harm of the last few days?" asked the Indian, with a troubled expression.

"Far more, for I am sure the timely news given to the lieutenant will save my people."

"And yet I was their enemy."

"And are now their friend. You lost your head in the frenzy that is spreading like a prairie fire among your people; your footsteps were guided by Providence, otherwise you would have missed the cavalry; they would have ridden to the ranch, and my folks would have been left as much without their help as though the soldiers had stayed at the fort. Besides," added the young rancher, "you can do as the officer suggested—show your own people the right course for them to follow."

"I will try," replied Starcus firmly; "I cannot understand how it was my senses forsook me, but they have come back, and," he said, with a meaning smile, "I think they will stay."

"I am sure of that, and you will do much good."

"Well, good-by," said Starcus, reaching down his unwounded arm. "I hope we shall meet again under pleasanter conditions."

Warren warmly pressed the hand and stood for a minute gazing after the strange fellow, who rode toward the nearest Indian village with the determination to carry out his new intentions.

It may as well be said that he honestly did so, and there is little doubt that his work was effective in more than one respect, and did much to ameliorate many phases of the sad incidents that speedily followed.

Left alone once more, the young rancher stood for some minutes in doubt as to his right course. It was idle to push on to the fort on foot, and he was at much disadvantage, now that he had no animal at command. He decided to follow the cavalry.

He had forgotten to ask Starcus how far off they were, but judged the distance was not great. The trail of the Indian's horse gave him the necessary guidance, and he broke once more into his loping trot, despite the rough nature of the ground.

A half-hour sufficed to take him to the scene of meeting, when he turned and began following the footprints of the horses at a faster gait than before.

Inasmuch as he was now a goodly number of miles from the bowlders where his friends were at bay before the attacking Sioux, he hardly expected to reach the place in time to take a hand in the decisive scenes or even to witness them. Starcus had left such accurate directions, and the Indian guides were so familiar with everything, that little delay was probable.

The distant sound of firing spurred him to still greater speed, and he ran so fast and hard that ere long he was compelled to drop to a walk to regain his breath.

Great as was his hope, he felt much misgiving. The cavalry might arrive in time, but in the flurry sad mishaps were probable. It might be that his father or mother or Dot or Tim had fallen before the vigilance of the assailants. He could not feel any real happiness until he learned beyond peradventure that all was well.

The shot fired by Tim Brophy the instant he caught sight of the warrior hurrying along the trail, with no thought that he was so close to the whites, was the best thing in every way that could have happened, for it not only wiped out the rash miscreant, but told those immediately behind him that the fugitives were at bay and ready to fight to the bitter end.

There was an instant withdrawal beyond reach of the rifles, of whose effectiveness they had received more than one striking example that night.

It took a considerable while for the Sioux to learn the whole truth. The fugitives had intrenched themselves in what was undoubtedly the most secure position near, and were on the watch. Gradually working round so as to enclose them against flight, the trail of the young rancher was discovered. A little investigation made known that he had mounted his pony and started off for assistance.

But help was no nearer than Fort Meade, and, as the Indians naturally thought, it could not possibly arrive before the morrow. If this were so, abundant time remained in which to encompass the destruction of the defenders. The Sioux decided to maintain watch, but to defer the decisive assault until late at night.

And it was this decision that saved the little party. Within the following two hours the friendly scouts reported the situation to the lieutenant of cavalry, who began his arrangements for an immediate attack upon the hostiles.

The latter, however, were as watchful as their enemies, and were quick to learn their new danger. They withdrew and disappeared after the exchange of a few shots, fired under such circumstances that no harm was done on either side.

The rescued whites were conducted to the foot of the ridge on the other side, where they were so disposed among their friends that all were furnished with transportation, and the journey to Fort Meade was begun, or rather resumed so far as they were concerned.

Not far away they met the young rancher, breathless and in an agony of distress. His joy may be imagined upon learning the happy truth. All were saved without so much as a hair of their heads being harmed.

The next day Warren returned for his pony, and found him so much better that he was able to walk with little trouble. The youth was too considerate to ask him to carry any load, and the two made the journey with the rider on foot.

And so it came about that Providence mercifully extricated our friends from the danger which threatened more than once the ruin of all.

THE END.